Best Friend,
Worst Enemy

Books by Beverly Lewis

GIRLS ONLY (GO!)
Youth Fiction

Dreams on Ice	Reach for the Stars
Only the Best	Follow the Dream
A Perfect Match	Better Than Best
Photo Perfect	

SUMMERHILL SECRETS
Youth Fiction

Whispers Down the Lane	House of Secrets
Secret in the Willows	Echoes in the Wind
Catch a Falling Star	Hide Behind the Moon
Night of the Fireflies	Windows on the Hill
A Cry in the Dark	Shadows Beyond the Gate

HOLLY'S HEART
Youth Fiction

Best Friend, Worst Enemy	Sealed With a Kiss
Secret Summer Dreams	The Trouble With Weddings

Best Friend, Worst Enemy

Beverly Lewis

2225

◊BETHANYHOUSE

Minneapolis, Minnesota

Published by Bethany House Publishers
A Ministry of Bethany Fellowship International
11400 Hampshire Avenue South
Bloomington, Minnesota 55438
www.bethanyhouse.com

Printed in the United States of America by
Bethany Press International, Bloomington, Minnesota 55438

Library of Congress Cataloging-in-Publication Data
Lewis, Beverly, 1949–
    Best friend, worst enemy / Beverly M. Lewis.
        p. cm. — (Holly's heart ; 1)
Rewritten version of: Holly's first love. Grand Rapids, Mich. : Zondervan,
c1993.
Summary: Thirteen–year–old Holly's relationship with her best friend Andie
is threatened when they both fall for Jared, the new boy in the seventh grade
and a fellow Christian.
    ISBN 0–7642–2500–6 (pbk.)
    [1. Friendship—Fiction. 2. Schools—Fiction. 3. Christian life—
Fiction.] I. Lewis, Beverly, 1949– Holly's first love. II. Title.
    PZ7.L58464 Bc 2001
    [Fic]—dc21   2001003809

Author's Note

I'm forever grateful to Charette Barta and Sharon Madison of Bethany House Publishers, who believed in Holly-Heart from her earliest beginnings, as well as to my superb youth editor, Rochelle Glöege.

Big hugs to my terrific teen consultants—Amy, Allison, Becky, Janie, Julie, Kirsten, Larissa, Mindie, and Shanna. Many thanks to my SCBWI critique group: Mary Erickson, Vicki Fox, Peggy Marshall, and Carol Reinsma. Other reviewers who offered valuable assistance are Barbara Birch, Barbara Reinhard, and Dave Lewis.

My sincere appreciation to Del Gariepy, who shared his medical expertise.

To Dave,

my heart-mate, best friend,

and very cool husband.

"Is it hot in here?" I whispered to the boy sharing my music folder.

Tom Sly's eyes bulged. "Holly Meredith, you're turning green!"

That's when it happened. Halfway through our seventh-grade musical, on the second riser, in front of half the population of Dressel Hills, Colorado, I felt dizzy. Faces in the audience began to blur. Heat rushed to my throbbing head. With a mouth drier than Arizona, I gasped for breath. Then my knees buckled and . . . I blacked out!

My best friend, Andrea (Andie) Martinez, witnessed this embarrassing scene and filled me in on the details later. She jumped off the risers and hightailed it over to help me. Tom Sly dragged me behind the risers and across the newly waxed gym floor to the janitor's room. Jared Wilkins followed.

When I came to, I was lying on the floor in the musty janitor's room. The first thing I saw was the adorable face of Jared Wilkins, the new boy. He smiled down at me, fanning me back to life with his music folder. In my half-dazed state, his blue eyes seemed to dance dreamily. *Maybe this fainting stuff isn't so bad after all*, I thought, squinting through the haze.

"Holly," Jared said. "Can you hear me?"

"Uh-huh," I whispered.

"Hang in there. Andrea went to get your mom." He glanced at Tom Sly, who leaned against the doorway, fidgeting.

Jared helped me sit up next to some mops and a bucket. I still felt a little out of it, but not so bad that I couldn't enjoy being the focus of his attention.

"Are you feeling okay?" he asked.

"I think so," I said weakly.

"That's good. You just take it easy till your mom gets here, all right?" Smiling, he sat beside me, leaning against the wall. "What a cool way to get out of a boring musical!"

"Speak for yourself," I said, feeling a bit stronger. "You didn't just faint in front of the whole school."

"But it's very romantic, being rescued by two men, don't you think?"

I was about to tell him that two seventh-grade boys didn't exactly qualify as men, but just then Mom and my little sister, Carrie, burst into the room, followed by Andie.

"Holly, honey, are you all right?" Mom leaned down to touch my forehead while Carrie frowned.

"I think she's going to be okay," Jared said, smiling at me. "It just got a little too hot up on stage."

"Well, let's get you out of this musty mess and into some fresh air," Mom said. "Thank you for your help, boys."

"No problem," Jared said.

Tom gave me a weird grin.

Mom led me down the hallway and settled me into a

chair in an empty classroom. Then she and Carrie went to search for a glass of water. As soon as they were out of earshot, Andie sat next to me. She twisted one of her dark curls around her finger. When she does that, I know something's up!

"Holly," she whispered, "you'll never guess what happened when you were out cold."

"What're you talking about?" I asked, still feeling a bit woozy.

"One of the boys tried to give you mouth-to-mouth resuscitation."

"What?" Suddenly wide awake, I grabbed Andie's arm. "*Who* did?"

She shook her head and looked away. "I, uh, shouldn't tell you."

"What do you mean *shouldn't?*"

"Oh, Holly," she whined. "I shouldn't have said anything."

I grabbed her other arm. "I *have* to know!"

She pulled away from me. "Don't do this, Holly."

"Do what? We're best friends, remember?"

She folded her arms. "I can't tell you."

"Why not?" I was desperate. "Did his lips actually touch mine?"

Andie nodded solemnly. "Your first . . . uh, kiss—well, not really—but, you know. And you weren't even awake for it," she said.

"Andie!" I howled. "Who was it?" I was dying to know, but just then Andie's parents poked their heads in the door.

"Ready to go?" Mrs. Martinez asked. "We told the baby-sitter we'd be back by nine."

"Okay, Mom," Andie said. Then she whispered to me,

"Call me the second you get home."

"Don't worry," I replied.

Mom returned with a glass of water and made me drink it. Then she held my arm while we walked to the car. Carrie opened the door for me. During the drive home, Mom kept pampering me.

"Are you feeling better, Holly-Heart?" she asked. Flicking on the inside light, she stroked the top of my head. "The color's returned to your cheeks. That's good."

Carrie giggled from the backseat. "You looked like a ghost up there."

"Did I? Did everybody see me faint?" I was mortified. Not only had I been semiresuscitated by a boy while unconscious, but a whole auditorium full of parents and kids had watched me keel over!

"Now, Holly, things like this can happen to anyone," Mom said. "There's nothing to be embarrassed about."

"But, Mom, that's not *all* that happened." Then I told her about the unneeded resuscitation.

"I think someone was probably trying to help you, Holly. That's all."

"But don't you see, Andie won't tell me who! I guess I wouldn't mind it if it was Jared, but Tom Sly, well . . ." I felt queasy at the thought.

Mom asked, smiling, "Does Jared happen to be the cute new boy you've been talking about? The one who spoke to me tonight?"

I nodded, and Carrie caught on and began to chant, "Holly and Jared, sittin' in a tree, K-I-S-S-I-N-G—"

"Mom!" I protested. I didn't need trouble from my eight-year-old sister, too.

"Carrie, *please*," Mom said.

I could hear Carrie snickering softly, but I let it go. It was enough for Mom to glare at her in the rearview mirror.

We pulled into the garage, and I could hear the phone ringing as we got out of the car.

"It's Andie!" I said, getting out of the car. I made a mad dash for the house and the phone. "Hello?"

It *was* Andie. "What took you so long?"

"Nothing," I said. "We came straight home." Quickly, I retreated to my favorite telephone stall—the downstairs bathroom. No one could hear me there. I lowered the toilet lid and settled down. "Okay, I'm ready for the whole story," I said.

She began to reveal what happened when I blacked out. Everything except the thing I was most eager to know. Then she said, "What do *you* remember about tonight?"

I was cautious, keeping the most private moments with Jared to myself.

"So . . . that's it?" she asked. "Nothing else?"

"Nope!" I said impatiently. "Now, when are you going to tell me who brought me back to life? You know, the almost 'kiss'?"

She sighed. "Like I said, I can't tell you."

"Why not?" I demanded.

"Honestly," she said, "I wouldn't keep my best friend in the dark unless—"

"Unless what?"

"Unless it's for your own good."

"Don't make me crazy, Andie. What good is not knowing?"

"My lips are sealed. True friends must shield one another sometimes."

"C'mon, don't get weird on me. Tell me!"

"I can't, I really can't."

"Okay, I'll just ask Jared. He'll tell me the truth."

"That's not a good idea," she said.

"Why not? He was there. He should know."

"You're getting too hyper, Holly."

"No kidding!" I was ready to pull my hair out. "Look, Andie, I refuse to talk to you until you tell me everything you know."

"But, Holly, I—"

"Good-bye, Andie." And with that, I hung up.

What a nightmare this was turning out to be. The most interesting thing that had ever happened to me, and my own best friend wouldn't even talk about it!

Fortunately, I had two whole days to get over my fainting episode. I would have died of embarrassment if I had to go to school the very next day!

I spent Saturday morning writing in my diary. Ever since third grade, I'd kept a journal. My secret wish was to be a writer when I grew up. That is, if I survived seventh grade.

My hand shook as I wrote the date: Saturday, January 16. Then I described the whole humiliating evening. Right down to Andie's awful secret. What *had* happened while I lay there, dead to the world? I imagined several scenarios and wrote them down. In one scene, Tom tried to get near me and Jared bravely pushed him away, protecting my innocent lips.

Carrie called up the stairs, interrupting my thoughts. "Holly! Andie's on the phone for you."

"Tell her I'm busy," I yelled back.

"She won't believe me!" she said.

I went to the head of the stairs. "Tell her I'm out."

"No, you're not."

"Okay!" I said, exasperated. "This is the truth: Tell her

I refuse to talk to her until she tells me in person what happened last night."

"Have it your way," Carrie snipped.

Tiptoeing downstairs, I observed my sister telling Andie what I'd just said. When Carrie hung up I asked, "What'd Andie say?"

"She said, 'Over my dead body,'" Carrie repeated, snickering.

I tromped back to my room. Enough of Andie's nonsense. "This means war," I muttered.

♥ ♥ ♥

At church the next day, I made a point of snubbing Andie. Sure, my conscience hurt when the minister talked about forgiveness, but I tried very hard to push the sermon out of my mind. I was still too upset to deal with it.

On Monday at school, I arrived early to Miss Wannamaker's gloomy English classroom, hoping to have the chance to talk to Jared or Tom. The walls in the classroom were a sick gray, a sorry color for a room where some of my best creative writing happened—assigned by one of my favorite teachers. Miss W was one of the largest women I'd ever seen, but she had the face of an angel and the heart of a saint.

The classroom slowly filled up, but before I could catch either Jared or Tom, Miss W herself arrived. "Dear class," she began, like a letter. That was her way. Every day. "Turn to page 249 in your literature books." She faced the chalkboard and wrote a "pithy" quotation, as she called it. The flap of skin under her arm jiggled as she wrote.

"Hey, Jared. How much to call Miss W the B word?" Tom Sly whispered behind me.

I glanced at Jared, who sat across the aisle.

"Do you mean . . . *blob*?" Jared blurted out.

Miss W whirled around. "Jared. Tom." They looked up from their desks, shocked. "You will both see me after class."

Her tone meant trouble—*big* trouble. I didn't feel sorry for Tom. His show-off routine had finally caught up with him.

But Jared? That was another story. . . .

Two months ago, right before Thanksgiving, Jared Wilkins had moved to Dressel Hills, our ski village nestled in the Colorado Rockies. I often caught him watching me. Of course, I sent zillions of encouraging glances right back. I secretly hoped *he* was the one who had come to my rescue, practically bringing me back to life like some fairy-tale prince.

"Dear class," Miss W began again, "I'm returning the quizzes from last week."

The papers came around. I got a ninety percent—not bad for last-minute cramming.

"Now for Thursday's assignment," she said. We all groaned, but she ignored us. "I want each of you to write a short story—two pages typewritten, minimum." More groans. "The main character must have something in common with you. Either your personality, hobby, or a special interest. Otherwise, the sky's the limit."

I jotted notes in my red binder and sneaked a look at Jared. He gestured that we should talk after class. I smiled yes.

Out of the corner of my eye, I saw Andie scrunch her

eyes at me like a snapping turtle ready to attack. I turned my back and ignored her. True to my word, I hadn't spoken to her all day—even though her locker was right next to mine.

After English, Miss W gave Jared and Tom a tongue-lashing. I waited in the hallway, nervously pulling on my hair. Who should I ask about Friday night? Jared or Tom? Tom was a tease and a real pain, but at least I'd known him since first grade. I hardly knew Jared at all. Thinking it over, I decided to play it by ear.

Before long, Jared came out. "Hope you aren't in trouble with Miss Wannamaker," I said.

"Not really, but Tom's still in there." He glanced over his shoulder, and then we headed down the hall toward our lockers. "Any chance you're going to youth group tomorrow night?" he asked.

"Well, Pastor Rob said he wants kids to wait till they're thirteen," I said, my heart thump-thumping.

"When will that be?" He reached for my books.

"I doubt you'll believe it if I tell you." I was actually walking down the corridors of Dressel Hills Junior High with the best-looking guy in school balancing my books on his hip!

"Try me."

"February fourteenth."

"You're kidding." He looked surprised. "Valentine's Day?"

"That's my birthday." My face felt like it had a bad sunburn. Jared must've noticed. He winked, which made it worse.

"How'd you end up with a Christmas name like Holly?"

Not waiting for the answer, he added, "I think 'Sweetheart' fits much better."

What was wrong with my knees? They shook like I was up on the second riser again.

"My mom named me after her great-aunt," I said. "We share the same name, but that's where the similarity ends."

"What do you mean?"

"My great-aunt Holly became a missionary to Africa."

"Really?"

"Her life was filled with fabulous excitement—dangerous adventure that would build your faith instantly. *I'm* lucky if I remember to read my devotions every day."

Jared grinned.

"Mom calls me Holly-Heart," I volunteered without thinking. "It's her special nickname for me, because of my Valentine birthday."

"It's perfect for you. You *are* all heart, aren't you?" His eyes softened.

I didn't dare tell him the nickname my gym teacher had chosen for me. Holly-Bones was verbal abuse at its worst, I thought, tucking my shirttail into the tiny waist of my jeans.

Arriving at my locker, we found Andie rummaging in hers.

"See you tomorrow," Jared said, handing back my books.

"Okay . . ." My heart pounded as he headed down the hall.

"Aw, how—what should I say?—promising," Andie muttered inside her messy locker.

Refusing to respond, I spun my combination lock and opened the door—right into Andie's.

"Ex-*cuse* me!" Andie said, pushing my door aside. Then she slammed her locker shut and stomped off.

I shrugged, deciding to keep my word about not talking to her. But I wanted to, so I could find out what she knew that I didn't. No way would I let her withhold valuable information from me—her best friend.

Suddenly Tom was beside me, hanging on my locker door. "That was some act you pulled last Friday night," he teased. "Some way to upstage the entire seventh grade."

"Maybe," I said, rummaging around my locker, pretending to search for something. Now was my chance to ask, but did I dare?

"You were so wiped out," he said, like he was dying to talk about it.

I summoned up my courage. "What happened after I fainted?" I asked. I kept my head in my locker so he couldn't see my flaming face.

"Are you saying Andie didn't tell you?" he said.

"Not yet."

"*Ve-ry* interesting." He put his hand to his chin and stroked an imaginary beard. "Hey, I guess you'll never know then. See ya." He waved and took off down the hall.

Weird, I thought. Why wouldn't he tell me? Sighing, I knew I had only one other option. Jared Wilkins. Now I'd *have* to ask him.

I walked home from school, watching my breath float ahead of me. As usual, Dressel Hills was swarming with winter tourists. Skiers roamed the streets and crowded into shops and coffeehouses. I turned the corner away from the bustling village, toward Downhill Court. The trees, bare as skeletons, shivered in the cold mountain air.

Picking my way along the slippery street, I thought of

Jared. Could someone that cute really like me? Could he overlook my "no-shape" and see my heart instead? Daddy had with Mom. She said she was so thin when they met, she looked like a pipe cleaner. As for me, I ate like a hippo, but nothing ever changed. Something about my metabolism made me burn up the fat. Meanwhile, all the other girls were changing . . . developing. Maybe something would happen in time for my thirteenth birthday—an eternal twenty-seven days from now.

I waved to a neighbor and plodded ahead to the tri-level three houses away, where I lived with my mom and sister. Flecks of powdery snow dusted the bricked icy walkway. I hoped we'd have another snow day soon. Andie and I always managed to get together on bad-weather days off school, no matter how snowy the streets were.

Then I remembered—she and I weren't talking. I kicked at a hardened gray clump of ice clinging to the gutter in front of our house. This secrecy stuff made me mad. Somehow, I *had* to get Andie talking again.

When I walked in the front door, Mom was relaxing with her usual after-work cup of peppermint tea.

I pulled off my shoes. "Love you, Mom," I said, tossing my scarf aside.

"Everything okay at school?"

I dumped my books on the sofa, scaring Goofey, our cat, away. "Andie's a total nightmare."

"What do you mean, Holly-Heart?"

"She *still* won't tell me who kissed me . . . uh, you know." I pressed my hands against my cold face. "Mom, I've *got* to know."

She nodded.

"I tried to ask Tom, but he wouldn't tell, either."

"What are you going to do now?" Mom asked.

"I don't know," I said glumly.

Three whole days had passed since I backflipped off the risers, and Andie still guarded her secret. I wondered if she'd paid the boys to keep their mouths shut, too. Sooner or later the truth had to pop out. Whatever it was.

After school the next day I studied at the library while I waited for Jared to get out of basketball practice. For once I didn't have to hurry home to be with Carrie, because she was going to a friend's house after school.

I couldn't exactly study, though. I kept looking out the window, across to the gym. I pictured Jared shooting hoops and dribbling up and down the court. I hoped I could actually muster up the nerve to ask him about the night I passed out!

Just then I spied him leaving the gym, wearing gray sweats, his navy blue gym bag slung over his shoulder. Even with his hair wet from the shower, he looked great. I jumped up and was out the front doors of the school in a flash.

Jared waved, coming across the freshly plowed walkway toward me. "Hey, Holly. Glad you waited." He grinned, like he was *really* glad. He held the door for me as we went back into the building. "Got time for a soda?"

"Sure." *Thump-thumpity* went my heart.

"Wish you didn't have to wait another whole month to

come to the youth group at church. I'll miss seeing you there tonight."

I breathed slowly, deeply. *Should I ask him about Andie's secret now?*

We stopped at his locker, and I waited while he grabbed his jacket and books. It was now or never.

I took a deep breath. "Jared, uh, can I ask you something kinda personal?"

"Sure, what?"

"I'm having a little trouble getting things straight."

He closed his locker and leaned against it. "What things?"

"Like what happened, you know, Friday night when I fainted?"

At that precise moment, Andie appeared. She marched toward us like a soldier in battle. Her dark eyes flashed. I tried to ignore her, but she came right up to me. "Holly, can I talk to you a minute?" she asked, oh so sweetly, offering a smile to Jared.

I was trapped. I couldn't be rude to her in front of Jared. What would he think?

"Excuse me," I told Jared. "Can you wait a sec?"

"No problem."

I pulled Andie over to our lockers. I'd vowed not to speak to her, and I wasn't about to now. She'd just have to read my expression. Pure disgust!

"What's with you?" she demanded.

Ignoring her, I reached into my locker for my jacket.

"Cut the jokes. Stay away from Jared," she said.

I scowled at her as I pulled my hair out of my coat collar and flung it over my shoulder.

"Talk to me." Her voice softened. "We're best friends."

My patience with her was almost gone. I glanced down the hall at Jared, who was still waiting for me. It was useless. I had to talk to her.

"Look, Andie, you've had your fun; you've played your secretive game long enough."

"Have you forgotten our Loyalty Papers?" she insisted.

" 'Course not," I said. "After all, *I* wrote most of them." In third grade Andie and I had drawn up our first Loyalty Papers. Every possible problem in our friendship had been thought out carefully and written down, legal-like. "Devoted, caring best friends, until the final end of us," was some of the dramatic wording. We revised the Loyalty Papers every year. But the message always remained the same—pals to the very end.

"Well, you're not following it very closely, are you?" she said, looking up at me. The top of her dark head just reached my shoulders.

"Hey, Holly!" Jared waved to me from down the hall. "Meet me at the Soda Straw later, okay?"

"I'll be there in a minute," I called, nodding. Then, as soon as he was out of earshot, I turned on Andie. "You're spoiling everything," I said. "Listen, Andie, if you hadn't shown up just now, I'd know your secret."

She began yanking all her stuff out of her locker, hurling books to the floor. It looked like the beginning of one of her fits. "I can't believe you asked him," she said over her shoulder. "You should reread our Loyalty Papers."

"I don't see what that has to do with anything," I said. "If you'd stop being so stubborn and just tell me—"

"Look who's being stubborn!" Andie interrupted.

"I should've known better than to talk to you." I slammed my locker extra hard and stomped off. Andie was being totally unreasonable, and I wasn't going to put up with it anymore.

Outside, the mountain air cooled me down some, but I was still steaming inside. Andie had never been so rude before, and we'd been friends for ten years—ever since preschool, where we became instant playmates. By first grade we were true-blue best friends, and that's how it had been ever since. We'd even traded favorite teddy bears! Her droopy-eyed Bearie-O had been sitting on *my* bed for six years. My hugging had worn the tan fur off his teddy head. And my beloved Corky sat with a collection of stuffed animals in *her* room.

Maybe it's time to send Bearie-O back, I thought as I opened the jingling door to the Soda Straw. It was a fifties-style diner, with red-vinyl booths, stools lined up at the aluminum counter, and a jukebox in the corner.

Jared sat in a booth toward the back of the restaurant, his notebook spread out in front of him. My heart did its skippy thing.

He looked up as I slid into the seat opposite him. "Still thirsty?" he asked, his eyes twinkling.

"Sure," I said. When the waitress came around, I ordered a pop.

Jared leaned forward, tapping his pen on the table. "Where were we . . . before, uh—"

"I'm sorry about that," I interrupted. "Thanks for waiting."

"Wouldn't have missed *this* for anything."

I felt my face grow warm. "Doing homework?"

"Just plotting my short story for English. Have you written yours?"

"Not yet." I couldn't tell him my mind had been focused on more important things . . . like him.

"I was worried about you the other night, Holly. You didn't hurt yourself, did you, when you fell?" he asked softly.

"No bruises." *Except to my ego*, I thought. Then the waitress brought my drink in a tall soda glass.

"Just glad I could help." Jared closed his notebook.

Reaching for my pop, I sipped through the straw. "Was I breathing?"

"You were breathing fine."

"Then why did I need mouth-to-mouth resuscitation?"

He smiled. "So . . . you heard?"

Br-ring! The bell on the door jingled as Andie appeared, popping my magical moment. Again!

"Hey," she said, bouncing over to our table.

Couldn't she read the secret message in my eyes? *Get lost. Get lost . . .*

Jared looked surprised. Her timing was unbelievable.

"Hi, I'm Andie Martinez," she said to Jared. "We met when Holly, uh, fainted the other night." She tipped an invisible hat.

"You two must be friends," Jared said, looking at me.

I wanted to say no, but told the truth. "We're best friends."

"Can I borrow her again?" Andie asked, pulling on my arm.

"We were just leaving," he said, grinning.

"Oh, were you headed somewhere?" she asked, her voice honey-sweet. Sickeningly sweet.

"Nowhere," I said. *Thanks to you.*

Awkwardly, Jared and I stood up. Looking into his face, I realized we were almost the same height.

Andie grabbed my arm again. "I need to see you, Holly. Alone." She mumbled something to Jared about being sorry and then promptly escorted me out the door and over to a clump of aspen trees. I was ready for a face-off like in ice hockey, only this was a game I wanted to end.

"What do you think you're doing?" I asked.

"I'm ready to talk. I'll fill you in on what happened Friday night."

"Finally! You've come to your senses." I glanced back at the Soda Straw. "So talk."

"This is it—the truth. Jared didn't try to revive you. *Tom* did."

I heard her words, but they made no sense. I wanted to turn her upside down like a salt shaker to get *all* the answers out.

"Why didn't you tell me in the first place?" I tried to erase the mental picture of Tom leaning over me, his breath on mine.

"You really shouldn't be so curious, Holly."

"Andie, give me a break."

"Figure it out," she said, her nose red from the cold. "We like the same guy."

"What?" I exclaimed. "Jared?"

She nodded.

"No wonder you're following us around everywhere," I said. "It's disgusting."

"Don't change the subject. There's more," she said, surprisingly eager to tell me everything. "Jared grabbed Tom off the floor—away from you."

Just as I had imagined it in my diary! "Really? What did he say?" I asked.

"His exact words: 'Get up, you total loser.' "

"He said *that?*" *This was too cool!*

"Jared knew you didn't need resuscitating. You were *breathing*. Tom jumped at the chance to get near your lips," she said, studying me.

I wiped my mouth on my coat sleeve, groaning. "I was probably his first romantic moment."

"Knowing Tom, that could be."

"So, you kept that part a big secret—about Jared pulling Tom away—because you didn't want me to know how Jared feels about me. Right?"

She nodded sadly. "It's just that I wanted Jared to like *me*."

"I should've known."

Andie's lip quivered. "Am I forgiven?"

"If you promise one thing," I said, forging ahead.

"What?"

"Ban the secrets, okay?"

"Sure, no secrets. But I can't promise much else."

I knew what *that* meant. The battle lines had been drawn. Jared was fair game. Not surprisingly, Andie and I had more in common than ever before. Only now instead of trading teddy bears, we were playing tug-of-war with a boy.

Across the street, Jared burst out of the diner and waved to us. He crossed the snow-packed street to catch the city bus. We watched as the doors closed, sighing identical sighs. This was too much!

"I wonder if he needs someone to type his English assignment," Andie said, breaking the spell.

"You wouldn't dare!"

Our eyes locked. Better than anyone else, I knew Andie

would do what she wanted. No one could talk her out of it. Not even her best friend.

"Well, gotta go," Andie said. "I've got youth group tonight—with Jared. See you later, Holly." She walked off, her curls bouncing.

I watched her cross the street and go into the drugstore. More angry and confused than ever, I headed for home. I wasn't quite sure what had just happened, but it seemed that I had traded the mini-problem of Andie's secret for a worse problem—the green-eyed monster. No way was Andie going to end up with Jared. No way!

When I arrived home, Carrie met me at the door. "Hi, Holly," she said, looking up at me with pleading eyes. "Will you French braid my hair?"

I sighed. "Okay, but let me grab a snack first. Where's Mom?" I poured some pop and threw together a peanut butter sandwich.

Carrie sat at the kitchen counter and banged her legs impatiently against the stool. "She'll be down. She already drank her tea. Guess you missed it."

It meant the first half hour of Mom's arrival home each day. She was usually cheerful even after a long day at work.

"How are my angels?" Mom said, coming downstairs a few minutes later. She was wearing the giant elephant slippers I had given her for Christmas.

I hugged her. "You look tired."

"I guess I am a little." She sat on the sofa, handing a yellow flyer to me. "This came in the mail today from church. It's information about a teen choir audition. They'll be traveling."

I clutched my throat—this was one of my dreams! "Do you think I could audition?"

"There's a good chance, honey. I'm sure the director will realize you're *almost* thirteen. Your birthday is so close." Mom flipped a page of the Psalms calendar on the lamp table. My birthday was marked with a red heart. It was going to be the best day of my life, if it ever arrived.

"When are the choir auditions?" I asked.

Carrie pulled me out of the living room, her pink brush and comb in her other hand.

"Next week, Tuesday," Mom said.

"I'm definitely going to try out," I called.

"C'mon, Holly, braid my hair *now*," Carrie said.

I reached for her brush. "Okay, let's do it."

Andie and I had learned how to French braid early in the fall of third grade. We'd visited her aunt's beauty salon one rainy day and had come home informed fashion critics.

Peering down at Carrie's thick golden locks, I remembered the first time I'd tried to braid her hair like this. It was four years ago, on the day Daddy moved out. Carrie was four, and I was eight.

I had helped carry Daddy's shoe boxes out to the car. I knew I shouldn't have tossed them in any old way. Lids and shoes scattered all over the backseat. Some helper I was. Daddy frowned at me for throwing them in. But I didn't care. That's how my insides felt—all scrambled up.

Inside the house, he put his arm around my shoulder. "Holly-Heart, you and Carrie can come visit me at my new place any time." With that, he kissed my sister and me.

"*This* is your place," I said. "And Mom's and mine and Carrie's!" It was weird—no one scolded me for yelling at him.

After Daddy closed the door behind him, I went over to Carrie, who sat huddled beside Mom on the couch. I took her hand. She followed me upstairs to the bathroom sink, where I wet her hair and tried the very first French braid. We could hear Mom's soft sobbing downstairs. *Things will never be the same*, I had thought. It was the worst day of my life.

"Make it tighter, so it won't come out." Carrie's voice pierced my thoughts. I pulled the strands carefully, making a perfect braid.

We didn't see Daddy after that. It frightened me. Things *weren't* the same. Eventually, though, things got better, little by little. Mom didn't cry so much anymore, and Carrie and I managed to live on without Daddy around.

"There you go." I finished off the braid with an elastic tie and a tiny ribbon. "You look fabulous."

Carrie ran downstairs to show Mom. I headed to my room to write the latest developments of my life in my journal. Andie and I were both interested in the same boy. That spelled only one thing: trouble ahead.

♥   ♥   ♥

During warm-ups in gym on Wednesday, Andie asked if I'd heard about the teen choir tryouts.

"Yep. Sounds exciting," I said.

"Pastor Rob told us about it after the youth service last night." She fluffed her hair, then twisted a strand of it around her finger. A bad sign.

"Jared and I signed up to try out," she said. "Too bad you're too young."

She acted like they were a couple or something—just

because they were both auditioning! "I'll be thirteen before the tour," I said.

But I felt left out. What if I wasn't allowed to audition? What if Andie and Jared *did* go on choir tour? I couldn't let myself think too hard about it. I just couldn't.

We practiced lay-ups, and Andie missed every time. When my turn came, I dribbled up and banked it in. There were a few advantages to being tall.

"Nice shot, Holly-Bones!" Miss Neff shouted across the court.

There it was—the dreaded nickname. Half the class snickered. It was true. I was bony all right, and there was no hiding it. I tugged on the back of my green gym suit. My stork legs barely filled out the baggy shorts. Mom had darted the suit to fit my waist, but she couldn't do anything about the hideous-looking wide-legged hems.

"Have you had your bacon and eggs today?" a curvaceous classmate joked as she dribbled past me down the court. I watched her move away gracefully. *Someday*, I thought. *Someday I'll look like that.*

"Each of us has a body clock," Mom had explained last year when we had our first heart-to-heart talk about womanly things. Trouble was, *my* body clock seemed to be losing time. And fast.

"By the way," Andie mentioned after showers, "Jared doesn't need someone to type his paper, but he *does* need an accompanist for his choir audition."

I whirled around. "You talked to him?" She was keeping her promise all right—no secrets between us. So how come it hurt when she told me everything?

"After youth group last night, he told me. And . . . he asked me to play the piano for him." Andie swaggered around, emphasizing her excitement. And her shape.

I couldn't compete with a fabulous pianist. Andie was moving in . . . fast!

After school I raced to my room to start the creative writing assignment for English. I titled it, "Love Times Two." It was about fraternal twin sisters who had nothing in common except the love of their lives. I wasn't foolish enough to give them names like Holly and Andie, but *I* knew what the story was about, and so would Andie and Jared. But the story was safe. After all, the story was for Miss W's eyes only.

"Hi ya, Bearie-O," I said, picking up Andie's old teddy bear. "Depending on how things go with your owner, you might not be here much longer. But before you go, you have to hear my side of the story." I began reading my first draft out loud. Halfway through the second page, Mom called from downstairs.

"Holly-Heart, Andie's here."

"Send her up," I called.

Andie dashed up the steps and plopped down on my canopy bed, snuggling with Bearie-O. "Ready to launch a writing career?" she said.

"A what?"

She slid a twenty-dollar bill out of her jeans. "You heard me."

I stared at the money. "What's that for?"

"For you, if you do a good job on my short story."

"You're joking, right?"

"Nope. I have to baby-sit my little brothers tonight. I don't have time to do the assignment."

"Andie, you know I can't do that. It's dishonest."

A frown sat on her forehead. "What'll I do? Miss W

will hang me from the ceiling if I don't turn in something."

"Maybe she will, but it still beats lying," I said.

Peeking over my shoulder, she asked, "What's *your* masterpiece about?"

I shoved it safely into a folder. "You'll never know."

"You were reading it to Bearie-O, weren't you?"

"Sure, I tell him everything. Same as you—just not this."

"You're hopeless," she said, pushing the money back into the pocket of her faded jeans.

"Pals forever?" I said with a shy grin.

"Some pal you are." She stood up to leave.

"At least I help keep you honest."

She scrunched up her face and said, "You really are Holly-Heartless." She closed my door with a thud.

Bearie-O took it all in. So did I. After all, I wasn't interfering with *her* first love. Just refusing to do her homework.

The next morning I hugged Mom before heading off for school. My clean hair smelled like roses under my knit hat. I couldn't wait to see Jared again. And to turn in my fabulous short story.

At last, English class! I slid into my seat and pulled my fiction assignment out of its shiny red cover. It deserved a top grade, no question about it. Surely Miss Wannamaker would recognize my amazing ability and my destiny . . . to become a famous writer. She might even wonder—as she read and graded the stories in the privacy of her home— from where in the world such a creative plot could have sprung.

"Dear class," she began as usual, "today we shall begin by reading our stories aloud."

I felt faint.

5

Miss Wannamaker's eyes skimmed over the desks. For a moment they stopped at mine. I held my breath. This was it, the end of life as I knew it. Someone sneezed behind me. Miss W looked up and miraculously called on Andie. I could breathe again.

Andie went to the front of the room. She opened her folder and began. "Once upon a year . . ."

I heard no more. If Andie picked me to read next, there were only about five minutes between now and a living nightmare! The similarities between my main characters, and the boy they liked, were too obvious. Could I change the story, making it up as I read aloud? Or become too sick to read?

My face burned with embarrassment as I thought how Jared would feel if I exposed our romance to the whole world. Jared Wilkins—my first real crush. I couldn't risk it. Not to mention Andie's fury when she discovered *she* was in my story, too.

The class applauded. Andie had done a quick job of it last night. At least she didn't get hung from the ceiling.

I'd rather hang than read, I thought as Andie's eyes

penetrated me. I quickly put my head down, avoiding her stare like a firing-squad victim.

Then I heard her say, "Jared Wilkins, you're next."

A truer best friend I could never have, I thought as butterflies played tag in my stomach. I listened intently as Jared read his story. It was unique and well written. About a mad scientist who met Einstein in a dream every night for seven days, and at the end, became not only sane, but wealthy from the secrets passed to him from the old genius himself.

Jared's story impressed me. We had more in common than I thought. I made a mental note to ask him about his writing ambitions.

The applause was loud; some boys whistled. Miss W frowned.

Jared's eyes scanned the classroom. He caught mine off guard. "I choose Holly Meredith," he announced.

A declaration to the world! Under any other circumstances, I would have been thrilled with his words. But now they felt like a punch in the stomach.

I stumbled to the front of the class. How could I have concocted a stupid story like "Loves Times Two"? I prayed for a miracle. If God could roll back the Red Sea for the Israelites, He could easily get me out of this mess.

I stated my title. Girls giggled; boys slouched.

"Excuse me, Holly, you'll have to speak up, please," Miss W said.

I smiled weakly.

Seconds from now I would reveal my dearest secret to the world, create more conflict with Andie, and maybe lose Jared forever.

I was well into the second paragraph of my emotion-packed composition when the school secretary tiptoed in.

All heads turned toward the door.

"The principal would like to speak with several of the students," she said politely.

Several turned out to be seven—all boys. Jared was one of them. This was it . . . my miracle! Jared would miss my true confession.

After the boys shuffled out, I continued reading with as little expression as possible, sneaking glances at Andie, hoping she wasn't paying attention.

Afterward, we passed our stories to the front. Miss W announced tomorrow's grammar quiz. And that was that.

I tried to dodge Andie in the hallway, but she caught up with me. I braced myself for the onslaught.

"What's up?" she asked.

"Not much." I smiled. Who cared if Andie creamed me? At least Jared hadn't heard my creative writing assignment.

"What are you so happy about?" she persisted.

"Let's just say God answers prayer."

"I know *that*. What else?"

I changed the subject. "Hey, looks like you got your story written without my help."

"I was up till midnight doing what you could've done in a few minutes." We waved at Marcia Greene, the brainiest girl in our class, as she passed us in the hall. Andie continued, "That was some fantasy you read today. It doesn't have anything to do with Jared and the two of *us*, does it?"

"Oh, you know how it is. We writers get inspiration from many sources."

"But did you have to describe me down to my toenails?" she asked.

"Hey, I do my best writing when it comes to things I know"—this in my most sophisticated voice.

"Don't you mean *people* you know?" She was accumulating ammunition. "Aren't you worried Jared will hear about it?"

"Who's going to tell him?" I said. "Besides, it's already obvious how he feels about me."

"Yeah, well, there're two sides to every story." She had that familiar glint in her eyes.

We came to our lockers. "Look at that," Andie said. There was a note, all squashed up, stuck in her combination lock.

I peeked over the top of her. "Who's it from?"

She opened it. "From Jared!" she crowed. "He wants me to practice the audition music with him after school tomorrow. At *his* house."

This was bad news. No, it was horrendous.

"He's heard I'm a piano whiz, no doubt," she bragged.

I opened my locker. No love notes for me.

"Want to tag along tomorrow?" she asked.

"No, thanks," I mumbled. "I promised Mom I'd watch Carrie after school."

"Holly." Andie's tone had changed. She sounded hurt. "Can't we be as close as we were *before* we laid eyes on Jared Wilkins?"

I looked at her. She gazed back with pleading puppy-dog eyes. I shook my head. "One of us has to back away from him," I said. "That's what we wrote in the Loyalty Papers: 'If we both like the same boy, one of us will give him up for the sake of our enduring friendship.' Can you give Jared up for the sake of our friendship?" I felt a giant lump in my throat. I didn't want to lose our friendship. But

I didn't want to walk away from Jared, either.

Andie grimaced. "It's time to revise those papers again."

"Why?" I asked.

"Might save our friendship, don't you think?"

The seriousness in her voice convinced me. "Okay," I agreed. "Saturday morning. My house."

Luckily the route to my next class took me past the principal's office. I was dying to know what had happened to the guys who were pulled out of Miss W's class. I rounded the corner to the principal's office. Three ghost-faced kids sat waiting for the principal. Remnants of my English-class miracle.

I spotted Tom Sly. "What's this about?" I whispered.

"Someone saw them smoking behind the gym at lunch," he said.

My heart sank. But I defended my crush. "Jared? Smoking? He wouldn't do that."

"Grow up, girl. Jared's no saint. Besides, lots of kids smoke . . . and more." He pulled me over against the wall. "Listen," he said in my ear, "can you keep a secret?"

"You can trust me," I said. But could I trust him? After all, he had tried to resuscitate me for no reason.

"I was the one who caught them smoking." He snickered.

"Who else saw them?" I asked.

"You're looking at him."

"Did Jared catch you spying?"

"No way."

"You're sure it was all of them? When was all this going on?"

"Hey, don't grill me, girl," he said. "During lunch. About twelve fifteen."

The principal opened the door of his office and out came a tall, muscular boy. It was Billy Hill.

"There's one of Jared's smoking buddies now," Tom said.

"Billy Hill doesn't smoke," I insisted. I watched him head down the hall, his shoulders slumped. He was one of the best players on the basketball team, and one of the nicest guys I knew. "Billy looks so helpless," I said as he disappeared from sight.

"Not as helpless as you looked after you conked out the other night."

I glared down at Tom, who was inches shorter than I.

"Your lips were so soft. We oughta try it again," he said.

He was actually admitting it. I gave him a dirty look. "You're disgusting."

"I was your hero. I saved you," he taunted.

"Jared was the *real gentleman*, dragging your face away from mine."

"You can do better than Jared." He cracked his knuckles one after another. "Like me, for instance."

"Don't be weird. We're barely friends." I tossed my head.

"I think you're gorgeous," he said.

Oh great, I thought, *not the class show-off.*

He must've seen me frown, because he blurted out, "Is it true what Miss Neff calls you in gym?"

I got away as fast as I could, but I still heard him calling after me, "Holly-Bones, Holly-Bones . . ."

The nickname stung all the way home. Still, that was nothing compared to the news about Jared. I couldn't wait to tell Andie what I knew, even if she *was* my rival.

I tramped up the snowy steps leading to my house. The porch swing swayed as I bumped past it. Daddy and I used to spend summer nights singing our hearts out on that swing. Sometimes Mom came out to join us, surprising us with iced tea to sip on between songs. But that was light-years ago.

Carrie met me at the front door. "I got an A on my math paper," she announced, waving it at me. A happy face smiled across the top.

"Great!" I congratulated her. "How about a snack?" I needed to get Carrie out of my hair so I could talk to Andie.

Once Carrie was safely settled at the table with apple slices, I retreated to the downstairs bathroom with the phone. I dialed Andie's number. Mrs. Martinez answered. No, Andie wasn't home yet. She was still at her piano lesson. "Please tell Andie to call back as soon as she gets home," I said.

I hung up and paced the house, waiting for Andie's call. Finally, I flopped in front of the TV beside Carrie.

"Where's Mom?" Carrie asked, snuggling with the cat. Goofey cleaned his little paws.

"She's working late tonight." I threw an afghan over our legs. "I hope she gets home soon. I'm starved." Actually, I wasn't super hungry. I just didn't like it when Mom wasn't home. I guess I worried too much. When she was gone longer than I expected, my brain kicked in with dumb things like *What would happen to Carrie and me if something happened to Mom?*

A half hour later we heard the garage door rumble open. Both of us raced to the windows and rubbed holes in the frost to peek out. Mom was home! Carrie and I raced through the kitchen to greet her.

"What do my darlings want for supper?" Mom asked as we hugged.

"I got your homemade pizzas out. How's that?" I said.

"Sounds wonderful." She removed her shoes on the way upstairs. "I'll make a salad in a minute." Mom looked worn out.

"*I'll* make the salad," I called up to her. She didn't answer. I hurried to preheat the oven. Then I pulled out a head of lettuce and began to shred it.

Carrie dropped a stack of letters on the bar. "Here's the mail."

I moved the mail to the desk in the corner of the kitchen. A blue envelope slipped out of the pile, landing on my foot.

I picked it up. My heart leaped as I saw my name written in bold black script. Who could it be? The handwriting wasn't familiar at all.

I checked out the return address. There was no name, just a street address and state. California? The last I'd heard, Daddy lived there. My heart began to pound.

The phone rang. I grabbed it off the desk.

"You called?" It was Andie.

"Yes, and it's real important, but I'm stuck in the kitchen now, so I'll call you after supper."

"Can't you tell me quick?"

"I can't talk now."

"Just give me a little hint," Andie begged.

"It's about Jared and—" I looked up to see Mom on her way downstairs. "I promise I'll call back later."

Quickly I hung up. Excited and nervous all at once, I

hid the letter in my pocket. Should I tell Mom? I would read it right after supper, then decide.

A letter from Daddy! This was headline news. Compared to *this*, the info about Jared was "Dear Abby."

6

"The pizza smells terrific," Mom said, sitting down at the table. I had drawn the curtains across the bay windows, and the dining room light threw a warm yellow glow across the oak table. The heat vent behind me blew warm air at my feet. Now that Mom was back, it felt like home.

We bowed our heads as Mom prayed over the food. Goofey rubbed playfully against my leg under the table.

"Long day?" I asked after the amen. Mom had pulled her hair back into a ponytail and scrubbed her face clean of makeup. Her eyes looked tired.

"Let's talk about *your* day, Holly-Heart."

"Well, to start with, you'll never guess what happened in English."

"Try me," she said, biting into a slice of pizza.

"I was reading my story about two girls in love with the same guy, when—"

"Now, Holly," she interrupted, "what kind of things are you writing for school assignments these days?"

"It's okay, Mom," I assured her. I could see this wasn't the time to share my English-class miracle with her.

Carrie jumped right in and began talking about her

math test. I knew my part of the conversation was probably over. Picking the black olives off my pizza, I tried not to think about the envelope that was poking into my leg through my jeans pocket. I didn't want to tell Mom about the letter. Daddy was probably the last person on earth Mom would want to hear from tonight.

"I saw your principal's wife at the post office this afternoon," Mom said, helping herself to another piece. "Was there some trouble at your school today?"

"Uh, yeah . . . kind of." I wondered how much she knew.

"Please, Holly, choose your friends wisely," she said. It was a definite warning.

"My friends are okay, really."

Carrie piped up. "Whose night is it to clear the table?"

"Yours." I pointed to her. "I made the salad."

"*I* set the table," she hollered.

"Girls, girls, please," Mom said. "Supper was wonderful, Holly-Heart. Do you mind if I go upstairs and rest?"

"Go ahead, Mom. Carrie and I will clean up the mess."

"We'll talk later tonight," she said, leaving the room.

Carrie and I cleared off the table and stacked the plates in the dishwasher. I wiped the crumbs from the counter and picked off the dried and gooey pieces of cheese from the oven rack. Meanwhile, the letter burned in my pocket.

As soon as we finished in the kitchen, I headed for my room. Closing the door behind me, I pulled the letter from my pocket.

I crossed over to my window seat and perched there, holding the letter in my hands. What would it say? Staring at the unfamiliar handwriting, I realized I wasn't ready to open it.

I hadn't seen Daddy since I was just a little girl. I'd never known what went wrong between him and Mom, and she never told me. Possibly thought I was too young. All I knew is that one day he had gone away, and after a few months, even his cards and phone calls stopped.

Soon after their divorce we started attending church. That's when Mom became a Christian. And then Carrie and I accepted Jesus, too. I couldn't remember seeing Mom happier. She was excited about her faith, reading the Bible and talking to the Lord every day. Our new church friends helped us put our lives back together.

Now, after four years without Daddy, my world was comfortable again. Safe. Somehow, I had learned to adjust. Praying helped. I honestly believed my prayers would help bring Daddy to Jesus. Wherever he was.

I held the letter—a window to another world. Did I dare open it? I hesitated. No, it was safer the way things were, with Mom and Carrie and me on our own. I started to rip it up. Then I stopped.

Curiosity won out. I tore open the blue envelope and pulled out a handwritten letter.

I could almost hear Daddy's voice as I read.

Dear Holly,

Perhaps you don't remember me very well. You must be quite a young lady by now. I would like to get to know you and your sister again. How do you feel about that?

I realize it's been a very long time since you've heard from me. If you find that you are interested in getting better acquainted, perhaps you could come visit me during your spring break. I have remarried, and my wife's name is Saundra, and she has a son named Tyler. They would also love to meet you. Take your time in deciding this. My address is on the front of the envelope if you want to write.

   I am sorry to tell you some sad news about your aunt Marla. She is very sick with cancer. I know she is one of your favorite aunts, and since she is my only sister, I wanted you to hear about this from me.

   I love both my girls. That may be hard for you to believe, but it is true. I would enjoy hearing from you.

                              Love,
                              Daddy

I stared at the letter. It seemed like forever since we'd sat on the porch swing, singing into the night. And the books. He'd read tons of them out loud to Carrie and me. At bedtime, after supper, on Sunday afternoons. Tears stung my eyes as I stuffed the letter, blue envelope and all, back into my pocket.

I tiptoed to Mom's bedroom, gently touching the door. Silently it glided open. I peeked in and saw Mom sprawled out on the bed. I crept inside and pulled the comforter over her. *She'll be asleep for a while,* I thought as I wandered downstairs.

Carrie was relaxing on the floor in the family room, drawing. She was surrounded by colored pencils, markers, and several coloring books.

"Carrie, this place is a disaster." I grabbed a handful of markers. "Can't you keep these in the box?"

She ignored me. "Is Mommy asleep?" she asked, playing with the red clippie on top of her head. Her blond fountain of hair gleamed in the lamplight.

"Mom's napping." I picked up a coloring book and started flipping through it.

"She's tired a lot."

"That's because she works with stressed-out lawyers all day."

"But why is she so sad?" Carrie looked up at me.

"I don't know." I wondered if Mom had heard about Aunt Marla. Maybe Grandma Meredith had called her. We were still close to Daddy's parents in spite of the divorce. Grandma and Grandpa had never really gotten over it. I remembered hearing Grandpa say, "Why is our son leaving his perfectly wonderful family?"

Guess we weren't that wonderful, I thought. Anyway, they still thought of Mom as their daughter. And Carrie and I would always be their granddaughters, no matter what.

The phone rang, and I ran upstairs to the kitchen to answer it.

"Hey, Heartless," Andie said. "How come you didn't call back?"

"Guess I just forgot." I kept my voice low. "Something really major just happened."

"What?"

"It's my dad. I got a letter from him."

"Really? Wow! What did he say?"

I told her all about the letter, how Mom and Carrie didn't know about it yet, and how he wanted to see me again. I even told her about Aunt Marla's cancer.

"That's really sad."

I swallowed the lump in my throat. "Yeah, I know."

There was a short silence. Then I changed the subject. "Did you hear why those guys got called out of class today?" I asked. "Tom says he caught them smoking behind the gym during lunch." I felt strange spreading this kind of news around, but I wanted to see if Andie would defend Jared the way I had.

"That's hard to believe," she said.

"You know what I think?"

"What?"

"I think it's one major mistake . . . or else someone's lying."

"There's one way to track it down." She sounded like a super sleuth. "Let's corner Tom at his locker tomorrow first thing, since he seems to know so much about it."

"Okay," I agreed. I wasn't so sure I wanted to talk to Tom Sly again, but with Andie around he'd never dare call me insulting names.

After I hung up, I pulled the letter from Daddy out of my pocket and folded it neatly. I went back down to the family room and curled up on my favorite spot on the sofa.

"Anything good on TV?" I asked Carrie.

Her eyes were glazed over. There was a Dairy Queen commercial on.

"Huh?" she whispered. I could see that the jazzy advertisement had won out over her drawing.

"Never mind," I murmured, reaching for my red binder containing every possible question on tomorrow's grammar test.

But I couldn't study. Instead, I daydreamed about the contents of Daddy's letter. I held the letter in my hand. It was strange reading his words, seeing his handwriting.

"What's that?" Carrie asked. The commercial was over.

"Oh, this?" I smoothed the wrinkles out of the California letter. "It's a letter from . . ."

Fast thinking required.

"Who?"

"From someone you really don't know." It was the truth. "I have to study now," I said, tucking the letter into my notebook.

"Hi, again," Mom announced, breezing into the room. She was dressed in her coziest pink robe, still wearing her funky elephant slippers. "Let's talk, honeys," she said, fluffing the couch pillows.

"Turn off the TV," I told Carrie.

"Come sit on my lap," Mom said to her. Goofey jumped on her lap, too. Mom leaned over and gave me a hug. "I've been thinking about someone very special lately," she began. "Do you remember Aunt Marla and Uncle Jack? And your stair-step cousins?"

I nodded. How could we forget the Christmas we spent in Pennsylvania two years ago? We'd chopped down a nine-foot giant of a tree. The tip of it bent under the lofty farmhouse ceiling. Our stair-step cousins—we called them that because each kid was a little older than the next—Carrie, Mom, and I took half the day to decorate the monstrous tree. It was great fun for all of us, except Daddy wasn't there.

"Your aunt Marla is very ill," Mom said softly.

"What's wrong with her?" Carrie asked.

"She hasn't been well for several months," Mom said, moving Carrie to the other side of her lap. "She has cancer. I've just heard from Grandma that some tests show Aunt Marla might not have long to live."

"I know about this," I whispered.

Mom peered at me curiously.

"Would you be surprised if I told you Daddy wrote to tell me about her?" I stared down at my hands, then up at her.

"Not too surprised," she responded. But her eyes said differently. "Grandma told me this news has changed your father."

I watched her face. "What do you mean?"

"Sometimes, when people learn that someone close to them is dying, it alters the way they view life."

"How?" Carrie asked.

"It makes them think more about how *they* want to live."

"I feel sorry for Uncle Jack and my cousins," I said.

"Let's pray that the Lord will give them extra strength during this painful time," Mom said.

We joined hands in prayer for Aunt Marla, Uncle Jack, and my cousins—Stan, Phil, Mark, and Stephanie. I prayed, too, that God would touch Aunt Marla and make her well again. Slowly, tears trickled down my face. The news about Daddy's letter and dear Aunt Marla all in the same day had caught up with me.

Mom wiped away my tears and looked into my eyes. "Do you want to talk?"

"I feel sorry for Aunt Marla. Very sad. And . . ." I drew in a deep breath. "Do you think I'll ever be able to forgive Daddy for leaving?"

"That troubles you, doesn't it, honey?"

I nodded.

"It takes a simple, honest prayer of forgiveness, and re-membering each day that Jesus does the same for us when we hurt Him," she said, taking my hand in hers and squeez-ing it gently.

"I used to miss Dad a lot." I looked away. "Then, when we didn't hear from him anymore, I figured he was gone forever. And now . . ."

"I know, honey." She leaned her head against me. "I know."

"You can read the letter," I offered hesitantly. It seemed like the right thing, letting her see it.

"Maybe another time," she said, her voice sounding stronger.

"Is it okay with you if I write back?"

"Of course. He's your father, Holly—that won't change. If you have a relationship with him, it's because you both want it."

Carrie had been listening to us silently, her eyes wide. "So *that's* what you were hiding before."

Mom intervened. "Maybe Holly will share it with you some other time."

"Did I get a letter, too?" Carrie sounded hurt.

"No," I said. "But Daddy says he wants to get to know you, too. I bet if you write him, he'll write back."

"Will Daddy start writing letters to Mommy?" she asked.

Mom said something that was probably pretty tough to say. "Carrie, love, your daddy is married to another woman now. He has a new family."

Carrie never understood all this divorce stuff. *Who does?* I thought sadly.

"Does he have some new kids?" she asked.

"He has a stepson."

"Will Daddy ever come visit us?" Carrie asked.

"If you see him, most likely it will be at his house," Mom said.

I couldn't believe she offered that. So I sucked in some air and dropped an enormous idea on her. "Dad says he hopes you'll let me fly out to visit him during spring vacation."

Mom sat motionless. "I'll have to think about *that*." She pulled us against her. "Now, don't we have homework tonight?"

While Mom coached Carrie with math flash cards, I tried to study for tomorrow's test. But all I could think about was Daddy. Did I really want to see him again?

My notes on adverbs blurred, so I set aside my English notebook. Other things seemed more important than maintaining my B+ average. Right now, anyway.

A few hours later I was propped up in bed, reading my devotional book without the usual suggestion from Mom. Bearie-O stared straight ahead as I tucked Daddy's letter inside my Bible, marking the verse for the day. It was Psalm 46:1. "God is our refuge and strength, an ever-present help in trouble." How did the writers of my devotional always seem to know the perfect verses to choose . . . for me? For today?

I slipped under my blanket and turned out the lamp beside my bed. Bearie-O fell forward, his face pressed against my lavender comforter. I leaned my elbow against his love-scarred head.

A timid breeze caressed the aspen trees outside my window. Through the window I could see the shadowy form of their bare branches. But try as I might, I couldn't see Daddy's face, his tall frame, or those gentle blue eyes in my imagination. Only the outdated picture on the nightstand came into view, faint in the twilight.

7

"Ready for action?" I asked Andie.

She nodded. We stood in the hallway before our first class, plotting our strategy. We had planned to corner Tom Sly and make him talk—whether he wanted to or not.

Andie grabbed my arm and we strutted down the school hallway, on our way to the stakeout.

"Super sleuths to the rescue!" I said.

We giggled.

"Got any spy glasses?" Andie said, peering around, her eyes squinting.

"Here." I handed her an imaginary pair, and she put them on with a flourish.

"Shh, there he is." Andie pointed at Tom, who had just finished unlocking his locker and was removing his jacket. "Remember, *I'll* handle this."

We strolled over and stood silently on either side of him. He slammed his locker shut and turned around. He looked surprised to see us, but he covered it quickly.

"Hello, beauties," he said, eyeing both of us. "How may I assist you today?"

"There's something we need to ask you," Andie said.

"We figured you'd be the one to ask, since you know everything about everyone around here." She laid it on thick. Boys fell for her routine, and since it worked, she kept recycling her approach.

"Since you put it that way," he said, "I'd be happy to fill you in. *Both* of you," he said with an endearing look at me.

He'd tripped over Andie's ridiculous line!

"So," she said, "what were you doing spying on Jared?"

That's it, Andie, shoot from the hip, I thought.

"Who wants to know?" he said, getting defensive.

"Let's put it this way. It's important," Andie said.

"What do you care?" he asked.

Andie was smart enough not to tell him we were both nuts about Jared. Or that we hoped to clear his name.

"He attends our church, and we thought—"

"You thought he was a good church boy, right?" he jeered. "Well, *nobody's* perfect."

"Christian kids have a perfect example to follow," I chimed in. "Like God's son."

"Oh, really?" he mocked.

Andie pressed on. "I thought I saw you in the gym watching intramurals yesterday during lunch."

"Well, you're wrong."

She turned to me. "Holly, you saw him there, right?"

Come to think of it, I had! He *had* been inside the gym the whole hour. I nodded.

"So maybe you didn't see Jared and those guys smoking at all. Right?"

"Back off. You don't know what you're talking about," Tom shot back.

Bingo! Andie, the genius, had touched a nerve.

And Tom looked guilty. I was beginning to suspect something was amiss.

"Guess we'll just have to get our information from a *reliable* source," Andie said.

"Excuse me, I have a class to catch." He shoved past us. We looked at each other and grinned knowingly.

"He's hiding something," Andie said, watching as he disappeared into a crowd of students.

"Definitely," I agreed. "Meet me at lunch?"

"Okay." And we were off to first period.

The morning dragged by. I could barely pay attention in history and math. The situations with Daddy and Jared weighed on my mind. I caught myself daydreaming several times.

When lunchtime came, I was nibbling on my roast beef sandwich as Andie came into the cafeteria, carrying her lunch tray piled high.

"Check this out," she said, balancing her tray on the back of a chair. "Jared gave me some of his leftovers. He said something about having timed tests in gym. Guess he didn't wanna pig out before the tests."

"Coach really puts the guys through the ropes on those tests," I said, remembering what I'd heard last year. I slid a piece of lettuce out of my sandwich.

Andie handed over a dish of apple cobbler. "Here, this is for you, from Jared."

"Jared?" I picked up my spoon. My cheeks burned.

"You're blushing," she sang.

He was thinking of me. Still, I worried. "Is this because he thinks I'm too skinny?" I asked.

"Think? Anybody can *see* that. But don't worry. Things'll change soon." She took a bite of her sandwich. "I can't wait till after school. Are you sure you can't come over to Jared's with me for the audition practice?"

I shook my head. I didn't want Andie to know, but I didn't like being around her and Jared at the same time. So I said, "I promised Mom I'd be home on time to be with Carrie."

On the way out of the cafeteria I ran into Jared. His eyes lit up, and he fell into step with me. My knees felt like jelly. Again. But all I could think of was how to bring up the subject of what had happened yesterday.

"Good luck on your timed tests," I said.

"Thanks. Did you get the dessert I gave to Andie?"

"I wasn't sure why you gave it to me."

"What do you mean?"

"I'm self-conscious about being thin." I looked away, embarrassed.

"Holly, I think you're *perfect*. Besides, I like tall, thin girls."

Good! That left Andie out. She was only four-feet-ten and a little on the chunky side.

"Are you ready to wow them at the choir auditions?" he asked, waving at Marcia Greene as she passed us in the hallway.

"I will be by the end of the week. Mom's going to ac-company me." I hoped he'd mention that Andie was ac-companying him, but he didn't. Maybe it was no big deal to him.

"Did you hear the choir's going to southern California?"

My heart jumped. That's where Daddy lived!

"Tough competition, too," he said. "Half the youth group is trying out, and there's only room for thirty."

"Guess we'd better get our voices in shape," I said. But

my mind wasn't on the auditions. I wanted to know the truth about what had happened yesterday behind the gym. We stopped near the entrance to the boys' locker room. If I was going to ask, I'd better do it now.

I took a deep breath. "Were you really smoking at the noon hour yesterday?"

"No way!" he said. "It was a complete setup. I was having lunch with my dad—you can't have a better alibi than that. Someone's trying to get me booted off the team, and I know who."

I thought I knew who it was, too. *Tom Sly.* "I bet he's threatened by the competition," I said, "and he doesn't want to share the accolades with some new kid."

"Right," he agreed, smiling. "Hey, where did you get the vocabulary?"

"From books," I said, realizing I was going to be late for home ec. "I devour them."

"Hey, I like that. By the way, I heard you wrote some terrific story for the assignment in English."

"I liked yours a lot. Ever think about becoming a writer?" I couldn't believe how much fun he was to talk to.

"It's one of my life goals," he said. "Did you have someone in mind when you wrote your story?"

Who had told him about "Love Times Two"? Surely not Andie. I played dumb. "What do you mean?" I said.

"Maybe we can talk about it sometime," he said, moving toward the locker room. "See you later," he said over his shoulder, flashing a grin that melted my heart.

"Set the record for the timed tests," I said.

"Thanks." He was about to push open the locker room door when he turned and said, "Holly, I'll call you tonight. How's eight o'clock?"

"Perfect," I said. I waved and took off down the hall before he could see the huge grin on my face. I kept smiling all the way from my locker to the home-ec room. I couldn't wait to tell Andie that Jared was cleared of the smoking charges. But the rest of our talk I planned to keep to myself.

I sprinted into class just in time. I settled onto one of the workstation stools just as Mrs. Bowen began giving instructions for the day's culinary creation: lasagna. When she finished, Andie made a mad dash for the sink and started to scrub her hands vigorously.

"Hey," I said, "we're making lasagna, not performing surgery."

Andie looked serious. "Tom manhandled my arm in the hall. He's ticked. Tried to get me to quit asking questions about Jared smoking. I'm scrubbing the contamination off me."

I laughed. "Jared's not even guilty, just like I thought."

"*You* thought? We both knew he was innocent. Did I miss some more important info?" She slipped a green-and-white terry cloth apron around her waist.

"Well, I just so happened to talk to Jared himself," I announced. "He's off the hook. His dad vouched for him, since they had lunch together yesterday. Besides, Jared says Tom's paranoid—thinks Jared will show him up on the team. Tom's been number one around here too long. Well, move over, number one, here comes Jared Wilkins!"

The girls at the next station were gawking.

"You must be having a personality change," Andie said, eyeballing me. "I've read about things like this. Love does strange things to people."

"My countenance shineth," I said, prancing around, waiting for the noodle water to boil.

"My friend needs help," Andie said to the other girls. "Come along, you poor dear." She led me back to the work station, pretending I was senile.

We fried up the ground beef and prepared the tomato sauce. After draining the noodles, we started creating the lasagna casserole layer by gooey layer.

"Whoops!" I almost spilled the tomato sauce.

"Watch what you're doing!" Andie warned.

My mind was on Jared. And Daddy's letter. I still couldn't believe my father had written to me and completely bypassed Mom. He'd overlooked the fact that she could easily veto his spring break invitation.

♥　　♥　　♥

A few minutes before the lasagna was finished baking, a siren rang out in the distance. Because of all the ski slopes in the area, we were used to this sound. But *this* siren, instead of fading away as it climbed into the mountains, grew louder and louder. It sounded like it was heading for our school!

Andie raced to the window. "An ambulance is parked out front," she said.

Mrs. Bowen went to the window, and soon we were all there, squeezing in, trying to see. "Look, Holly!" Andie said, pointing at a woman. "I think Jared's mother is down there."

"How do you know it's her?" I asked.

"I saw her in church last week. What's *she* doing here?" Andie stared at me, her face filled with fear.

Pressing my nose against the icy window, I saw a white

stretcher emerge from the ambulance. Two men wheeled it into the gym entrance. "Something terrible has happened," I whispered.

Minutes later, there was more commotion. Now the stretcher carried a tall, brown-haired boy wrapped in wool blankets.

It was Jared. Was he alive? Mrs. Wilkins stepped inside the ambulance. The doors closed.

My heart sank as the siren sang its mournful song.

8

The ambulance was long gone when I backed away from the window. I wandered over to Andie, a huge lump in my throat. She had removed the lasagna from the oven and was staring down at it sorrowfully. The cheese was brown and some of the noodles were burned black around the edges.

"I feel sick," I said, holding my stomach. "And not because of the ruined lasagna."

"I can't believe this!" Andie cried. "We have to find out what happened."

"Someone next period might know something," I said. "I'll probably bomb for sure on the English test next period."

Andie pushed the chairs under the tables. "Who cares about English tests—Jared's been hurt!"

Tears blinded my eyes.

The bell rang as Andie put her arm around me. "Let's go to the rest room. We'll pray in there," she whispered.

I gathered up my books. Andie led the way to the bathroom. She always seemed stronger in situations like this, even when we were little girls. For me, the tears came all too quickly.

"C'mon, let's pray," Andie said, grabbing my hands. I balanced my books on the sink. Andie's prayer was long and fervent. When we opened our eyes she looked up at me, poised for action.

"Here's the deal," she said. "After school we split to my house and get Mom to drive us to the hospital."

"Okay," I said, "but I'll have to call my mom first."

A toilet flushed. The serene moment gushed away. An astonished girl came out of the stall. I guess she'd never heard anyone pray out loud. And in school, too. She turned to stare at us before making her departure. We smiled back.

"I feel better," I said.

"Me too," Andie said. We headed for English in silence.

Settling in for the test, I noticed Tom Sly and Billy Hill were missing. Rats! No chance to ask about Jared and what had happened in gym. During timed tests today.

My stomach churned. I felt as prepared for this test as a computer without a printer. The short time I'd spent studying wasn't going to earn me the kind of grades I was used to getting.

The questions on the test blurred as I thought about Jared in the hospital.

Hospital. A scary thought. It reminded me of Aunt Marla. She was dying! My favorite aunt. It wasn't fair. She was so cool—always doing terrific things for Carrie and me, spoiling us when we went to visit at Christmas and in the summer.

Just then, Marcia Greene, the smartest kid in class,

brushed past me on her way to Miss Wannamaker's desk. She'd already finished the test! Daydreaming was a luxury I couldn't afford. I gripped my pencil and filled in some answers.

After class Andie and I hung around until two boys who had been in gym during last period finished talking to Miss W. Then we headed for them like vultures.

"Hey, Jeff, do you know what happened to Jared Wilkins in gym?" Andie asked.

"Yeah," Jeff Kinney said. "He fell off the trampoline during warm-ups for timed tests."

"He was up really high," Mark Jones added.

"What happened?" I asked.

"He lost his balance and fell. The bone was sticking out of his leg," Mark said.

"I hope he won't have to have surgery," I said.

Mark shrugged. "Beats me."

"C'mon, let's go," Andie said, pulling me away. We turned and headed down the hallway.

I held my books tightly against my chest. "Mark's attitude is sick."

"You got that right."

I didn't get it. "What's the entire male population of the school have against Jared, anyhow?"

"You've seen how new kids get treated around here. We're a bunch of snobs," Andie said.

"But the guys must be *jealous* of Jared. For once here's a guy who has more than muscles and good looks. He's got smarts, too."

Andie nodded, then gave me a fierce look. "I have a feeling Tom Sly knows something about Jared's accident."

She jammed her books into her locker. "And I intend to find out what."

♥   ♥   ♥

At Andie's house, the smell of brownies lured us into the kitchen. Mrs. Martinez looked similar to Andie, with dark curly hair and sparkling eyes. "Brownies, girls?" she asked.

We plopped down at the bar while Mrs. Martinez cut two large pieces.

"Mom, there's been an emergency at school," Andie blurted out. "Can you take us to the hospital?"

"What's wrong?" her mother asked, pouring a glass of milk.

I spoke up. "We want to go see Jared Wilkins. He's been hurt."

"What happened?"

We explained what we knew of the accident, and Mrs. Martinez listened sympathetically. But at the end she shook her head. "I think the two of you should stay put and pray for him instead. I doubt you could see him now anyway," she said.

Andie's curly-haired twin brothers bounced into the kitchen. Seeing the treats, they tripped over each other to get to us.

"Me get tweet?" one of the two-year-olds asked.

"Yes, Chris. You get treat," Andie said, pulling the pan of brownies closer. She cut a small piece for each of them. Chris and Jon jammed the brownies into their mouths and went running around the kitchen. Mrs. Martinez followed them to make sure they wouldn't make a mess of things.

"Still want to get together tomorrow?" Andie asked.

"What for?" I'd completely spaced out.

"The Loyalty Papers, remember?" Andie said. "We're going to revise them. And now that I see how much we both care for Jared, I think it's very urgent."

Andie's comment confused me. I thought things were actually improving between us.

Just then I remembered something else. "I forgot to call Mom." I hurried to the wall phone and punched in the number for her office. She answered almost immediately.

"Mom? I'm at Andie's. I didn't go right home because there's been an accident. . . . A friend of mine was hurt at school."

There was a pause; then Mom, sounding quite displeased, said, "Holly, your sister's been home alone all this time. Usually you're more responsible than this."

"But I *had* to come straight to Andie's house," I said, defending myself.

She didn't buy it. "You should've called. I'll phone Carrie to let her know you're on your way."

She hadn't even asked about the accident. All she cared about was Carrie, who was perfectly able to take care of herself. Frustrated, I said, "I don't need a lecture about this, Mom. I really don't." I hung up without saying goodbye.

When I arrived home, Carrie was watching cartoons. "How was your test today?" she asked.

"Probably flunked it," I told her. "Where's Mom?"

"She's home now, and boy, are you in trouble."

"Why?" I slouched into the arms of my favorite sofa.

"Something about your disrespectful back talk." Carrie

was sounding like a grown-up. Too big for her britches.

"Guess I should go up and apologize," I complained. I stood and trudged up the stairs. Mom's bedroom door was closed. I knocked and waited.

"Come in," she said.

Not daring to look at her, I plodded over to the bed and sat down. The first few seconds were tense. Then she put her arm around me. "I love you, Holly-Heart, you know that."

"Mom?"

"Yes, honey?"

"It's getting harder to be . . ." I didn't know how to tell her that I was feeling more and more rebellious—at least sometimes. "To be obedient."

She smiled knowingly. "There are hundreds of changes occuring in your body right now. Your emotions will fluctuate, swing up and down. And most of the time, you won't understand why you're feeling the way you are."

"So this will happen more and more?"

"It's part of becoming a woman," she said.

I picked up the rose-colored potpourri pillow on her bed. Hugging it against my flat chest, I breathed in its sweet fragrance. "I was very sassy on the phone. I'm sorry, Mom."

"I forgive you, honey. We all have moments like that. Try harder next time."

I sighed, feeling exhausted. "You won't believe what happened at school today." From then on it was like opening a can of soda. My words poured out. I could always talk to Mom. The fiery rebellion was gone.

After supper we got a call from the church prayer chain. The actual facts: Jared was stable, but he was suffering some momentary amnesia from having struck his head on the hard gym floor. As for his leg, it would be in traction until they operated. Then he'd be in a cast for a month or so.

So much for basketball this season, I thought. I was disappointed for him. And I was dying to see him.

"When can I visit him?" I asked Mom while I washed the pans. Carrie was drying, and Mom was putting away the leftovers.

"We'll have to call the hospital and see about visitation," Mom said.

Carrie teased, "Maybe his amnesia wiped *you* out of his memory forever."

"No chance," I said, flicking her with soap suds. "I'm unforgettable."

When the phone rang, Mom answered it. We could tell by Mom's responses that the call was from Grandma Meredith. Carrie and I looked at each other, then watched Mom anxiously. Her smile faded, and the lines in her forehead deepened as she listened. Finally, she said, "I can't leave the girls, but I wish I could help in some way." She sat down slowly.

There was a long pause.

Mom leaned her blond head against her hand. When she spoke, it was barely a whisper. "Please tell Jack and the children we're praying." Hesitantly, she beeped off the cordless phone.

Carrie and I stood like statues as Mom searched for a tissue in her pocket. Neither of us dared speak.

"Darlings," Mom began slowly, "Aunt Marla's not doing well. The docs think she has only a few weeks left. . . ." Her voice broke.

We knew.

Later that evening, when we'd rehashed the news of Aunt Marla's cancer, Mom and I made a feeble attempt to rehearse my audition piece for the youth choir. Mom made tons of errors, and it was obvious her heart wasn't in it.

In bed—hours later—I read out loud to Bearie-O. Having him close reminded me of the special friendship Andie and I had shared all these years. But lately things were so up and down between us. Like a yo-yo, or worse.

I continued reading, but my concentration was messed up. Uncle Jack and my cousins kept creeping into the mystery novel I struggled to read. What would they do if Aunt Marla died? My worries wandered in and out of the story.

Daddy strolled across chapter three. What about a response to the spring break question?

Jared called to me from chapter five. His leg had to be amputated.

In chapter six, Andie demanded a major overhaul of our Loyalty Papers.

Halfway through chapter eight, Carrie threatened to whack off her long hair. She was sick of my sarcastic remarks and didn't want to look like her big sister anymore.

It was close to midnight when all of them finally faded away. And I fell into a restless sleep.

9

The next morning I slept till nearly nine o'clock. Mom was relaxing with the paper when I wandered downstairs. "Good morning, Holly-Heart," she said, glancing up from the sofa. "Ready for breakfast?"

"Definitely." I was starving as usual. So Mom fixed a platter full of pancakes with scrambled eggs on the side, then sat down with me to chat.

"Can I make snickerdoodle cookies after lunch?" I asked. "Andie's coming over later. She wants to revise our Loyalty Papers, and I want to make sure she's in a good mood, you know."

"Sounds like you're going to bribe her." Mom's eyes twinkled.

"Not really." Quickly, I changed the subject before too many questions were asked. "Where's Carrie?" I said, finishing off my last bite of eggs.

"Watching TV," Mom said. She sipped her peppermint tea, her hands wrapped around the mug to warm them.

"Did Carrie say anything to you about cutting her hair?"

A shocked expression crossed Mom's face. "No . . . this

is the first I've heard of such a thing. Why do you ask?"

"Just checking," I said, recalling the parade of problems dancing across the pages of my book last night. But the problem I cared about most was Jared Wilkins.

Thankfully, Mom didn't probe any further about Carrie chopping off her hair. After we finished cleaning up the kitchen—and Mom was safely out of the room—I dashed for the phone and called Andie.

"Hi." She sounded alert and ready for action.

"Whatcha' doing?"

"This is so cool, Holly. Listen—I just found out, Jared's parents agreed to let me bring my keyboard to his hospital room."

"What for?" I asked but guessed what she was up to.

"The youth choir director wants to audition him at the hospital."

There was a long silence while I groped for something to say. Andie had one-upped me, and I knew it.

"Sounds . . . well, interesting," I said at last. The old green-eyed monster was poking its nose into my business again. "He must really want Jared in the choir."

"Good tenors are hard to find," she said.

"What about Jared's amnesia?"

"It's simple. He doesn't remember anything that happened yesterday."

"Nothing?" I thought about the phone call he'd promised to me. "What about the fall off the tramp?"

"Nope, not even that."

"How do you know all this stuff?" I asked.

"My mom and his mom talked."

Real sweet, I thought.

"When are you going to practice the song with him?" I

was dying for her to ask me to go along.

"Tomorrow afternoon. He's supposed to rest during the morning. Which is probably a good idea. He's in traction, you know."

Her know-it-all attitude irritated me, but I said, "Still coming over today?"

"Yep. We've got major work to do on the Loyalty Papers, remember?"

Of course I remembered, but I secretly hoped *she* had forgotten. "Are you sure you want to revise them?" I asked.

"Sure do! Got 'em ready?"

"Uh-huh," I said, giving in. "The Loyalty Papers await. And I'm making snickerdoodles after lunch. Wanna help?"

Andie said, "I'll help by making them disappear."

"Fabulous," I said, and we hung up.

But I was worried about revising the Loyalty Papers. Really worried. I felt sure that the restructuring of our original documents—made between friends—might cause another major argument, especially since Andie and I were both crazy over Jared.

Upstairs, I showered, then dressed in my most comfortable jeans with frayed hems, and my favorite old T-shirt. Counting the days till my birthday was priority on my morning agenda. In giant numbers I wrote *22 days* on the scrap paper stuck to my bulletin board. The day still seemed too far away to plan my big bash.

❤   ❤   ❤

After lunch I mixed together some flour, cream of

tartar, soda, and salt. Then I stirred in soft butter, sugar, and eggs.

Andie arrived just as I began rolling the dough into walnut-sized balls. "Mmm, yum!" she said, eyeing the cookie sheet.

"They'll be ready to eat in about eight minutes," I said. "Want some apple juice while we wait?"

"Thanks," Andie said, watching as I poured the cold juice.

Then, flicking on the oven light, we watched the snickerdoodles do their thing—puffing up at first, then flattening out, leaving a crinkled top. After they were done, we let them cool. Then, piling the cookies high on a plate, we headed for my room with plenty of sweet treats to munch on.

Andie plopped down on a corner of my bed. "Ready to revamp the Loyalty Papers?"

I was glad she couldn't see my scrunched-up face as I sorted through my dresser drawer, searching for the precious papers. Then I spied them in the legal documents holder Mom had given us years ago. The folder was a reject from the law firm where she worked as a paralegal.

Overly eager, Andie set the plate of cookies in the middle of the bed and began to shuffle through our papers. As she read, she reached for a snickerdoodle cookie.

I, on the other hand, sat on the opposite side of the bed and nibbled on my cookie, watching her face for any warning signs.

She frowned. I gulped.

"Look here," she said. "We really missed it on *this* paragraph." She pointed to the page, clearing her throat like the principal getting the kids' attention in assembly. "Page three, paragraph seven." She paused. "This is really absurd, Holly."

"What is?" I peered down at the page between us.

"This dumb idea . . . that one of us has to back away from a boy if the other person likes him, too."

"Well, we wrote that two years ago, before Jared ever appeared on our scene. Maybe we should add something about whoever likes the guy *first* gets dibs," I suggested.

"Oh no, you don't. That'll never work. Besides, how could we know for sure who liked him first?" She flipped through the next two pages. "Were we so naïve to think we'd never attract the same boy?"

"Well, look at it this way," I said, trying to remain calm. "Since we're both so different—in looks, in personality, in the way we think—maybe we were on to something when we wrote that part."

She stood up, brushing the cookie crumbs onto the floor. "I'm sick of your logic, Holly. Maybe we should talk about this some other time, when you're thinking clearly."

"Wait!" I followed her out of the room. "What's wrong with my idea?"

She glared at me. "Don't be dense. Neither one of us is going to back off, and you know it." She was in the hallway now, heading for the stairs.

"Where are you going?"

"Home—to practice Jared's audition music. See you, Holly. Thanks for the snickerdoodles."

A lot of good the snickerdoodles did. Back in my bedroom, I stared glumly at the plate. One lone cookie was left. I picked it up and ate it. Without licking my fingers, I shuffled the pages of our Loyalty Papers. Who cared if they got messy. They were useless now.

At last, I set off for the lower-level family room. There, I joined Carrie for a DVD cartoon, trying to get both Andie and Jared off my mind. But nothing could stop me from thinking about Jared—hurt and alone—in a hospital room.

After the cartoon, I purposely grabbed Mom's attention by juggling four cookies at a time. When I quit showing off, the kitchen floor was a crumby mess. Goofey licked up the sweet crumbs.

"Something's *really* troubling you, Holly," Mom said, handing over the broom to me. "You're not yourself."

"It's Jared. No . . . it's Andie. She and I both like Jared. And now *everything's* a disaster."

Mom thought a moment; then she said, "Why can't the three of you be friends?" She said it so innocently, I thought surely she must be joking.

"It doesn't work that way."

"Well, enlighten me," she said, rinsing out a rag for me to wash the spots off the floor.

I got down on the floor, scrubbing up the mess I'd made. "I think Jared wants me to go with him, and Andie's totally freaked out about it." I looked up at her from all fours.

"Go with him . . . where?"

"Nowhere, Mom." This was hopeless. "It's just an expression—doesn't mean dating or anything. It's just when a guy likes a girl and wants her to hang out with him at school and church and, well, you know." I got up and tossed the dirty rag into the sink.

Mom was studying me. Hard. "Hang out, you say?"

"Right."

"I see," she said. But of course she didn't. The days when Mom was a teen were long past.

Later in the afternoon Carrie and I tagged along when Mom went grocery shopping. At the check-out, we bagged the food for her, racing to see who could get the most in each bag.

"Oops, this isn't working," Carrie said, bending over to retrieve one of the grocery sacks. Then two boxes of microwave popcorn tumbled out.

"Look out!" I cried as two oranges found their freedom, rolling under the counter.

The clerk announced the grand total, casting a peculiar look and a frown at Mom.

"Big mistake bringing *you* along," I told Carrie as I reached around the back of the counter, groping for the oranges.

"Mom! Holly's being a pain," Carrie whined.

Mom looked frazzled with stress. "Please go and wait in the car." She dangled the car keys in my face.

"Send Carrie. This is all her fault." I glared at my sister.

"I want *you* to go now," Mom said again.

"Perfect," I whispered.

Outside in the cold car, I turned on the ignition. Grandpa Meredith had let me start his car last summer when they came to visit. I'd even backed it in and out of the driveway dozens of times.

Shivering, I stayed seated in the driver's seat and turned on the heater full blast. The lights of the village began to twinkle on as dusk approached. Mom had no right to send me out here this way. What had I done to deserve such treatment?

Pulling a tablet out of the glove compartment, I began to write: *Dear Daddy*. It was time for an answer to his invitation. Way past time.

When I saw Mom and Carrie coming toward the car with the groceries, I scrambled over the front seat and sat in the back, hiding the half-written note in my coat pocket.

Mom doesn't need to know about this, I thought, feeling sneaky and good about my secret.

♥ ♥ ♥

The next day was Sunday. Once again, I had trouble concentrating on the sermon. Andie, who was sitting across from us, next to her parents, looked much too confident. Her brunette hair, perfectly in place, framed her round face. Oh, I could just imagine her playing the piano for Jared, their eyes catching snatches of unspoken adoration. It was unbearable, so I tried my best to block out those kinds of thoughts.

In my Bible, I underlined the pastor's text with a red pen. Carrie cozied up to Mom in the pew, and I wanted to be somewhere else. Somewhere like the Dressel Hills Hospital, maybe in traction in the room with Jared.

I knew there was only one reason why Andie hadn't asked me to go with her to Jared's audition: She wanted all his attention. Some best friend she'd turned out to be.

Just then Carrie peeked around Mom in the pew and flashed me a less-than-angelic grin. Her missing teeth completed the impish look.

Most of the time I loved Carrie, but sometimes I felt that Mom spoiled her rotten. Getting away from my little sister for a full week during spring break was a fabulous thought. And if I got permission to go to California to visit

Daddy, I'd be leaving Andie behind for a while. It seemed, now that I thought of it, there was only one person I would miss at all. Jared.

When we arrived home and sat down to dinner, the food tasted blah. Usually I can't get enough baked chicken and onions, but Jared was on my mind and in my heart.

Later, after the dishes were stacked in the dishwasher, Mom grabbed a note pad and sat at the table. "Let's plan your birthday party, Holly-Heart."

I glanced at the calendar. "It's still too far away."

"Oh, but the days are flying by," she said, clicking the pen. "How many friends do you want to invite?"

I paused to count. "I can think of at least ten."

Her eyebrows rose high above her eyes. "Well, I was thinking more in terms of seven. Including you, that's eight. An even number is always nice . . . for games and things."

Then I said something I shouldn't have said. And in a catty sort of way. "Who cares about even numbers?"

Mom sighed. "Maybe we should talk about this later." She was exasperated with me, and how could I blame her? I'd given her a tough time on purpose.

"Why don't we just forget about this birthday? Maybe turning fourteen next year will be better!" I stormed out of the kitchen, certain that Andie was doing her musical thing right now at the hospital with Jared. More than anything, I wanted to be there. Not *here*.

Upstairs, I curled up in my window seat and wrote the remainder of my letter to Daddy. I tried to imagine what his new life was like. This, after all, was *his* house. He and Mom had fallen in love with Colorado. They'd moved from Pennsylvania after getting married, making a life together in this skier's paradise. And what a skier Daddy was! He even gave me skiing lessons, starting when I was five. After a few practice runs, the sport was like breathing. Daddy said I was a natural.

Surely his new life wasn't half as good as it had been here with us. And what about this new stepson of his? Somewhere out there I had a nine-year-old stepbrother. How weird was that?

A knock on the door interrupted my thoughts. Mom poked her head in the door. "Holly-Heart, Andie's on the phone."

My heart skipped a beat. *News about Jared! Could it be?*

"I'll get it up here," I said, coming out of my room and going to the hall phone. "Hello?"

"Hey, Heartless, still speaking to me?"

"Why shouldn't I be? *You* were the one who stormed out of here yesterday."

"Well . . . Jared had his audition."

"How was it?"

"Jared's voice is as fine as he is."

"I *know* that. How's Jared *feeling?*"

"Feeling? Well, uh, I know you won't believe this, but our hands touched today, when no one was watching. Is that what you mean?"

"You are so not telling the truth," I said.

"Hang on, I'll get Jared to tell you himself."

"You're disgusting, Andie," I yelled. "And you call yourself my best friend? I'm tearing up the Loyalty Papers. They don't mean anything to you anymore."

"Holly, what's going on?" she said, acting innocent.

"You're ruining my life."

"What's happened to you? You've changed so much.

Honestly, I thought you'd be happy for me . . . for us." She was pouring it on like honey, though her words were anything but sweet.

"You want me to congratulate you for stealing my boyfriend?" I yanked at my shoe strings.

"But you weren't really—"

"This is truly the end of our friendship," I said, kicking my tennis shoes down the hall.

"You'll change your mind if you want to be on choir tour."

"Meaning what?"

"The director told us—Jared and me—about the theme for the tour. It's unity. 'Our hearts in one accord,' Mr. Keller said. You know—getting along. Which doesn't allow for fighting over boys or anything else."

I'd had it with her preaching. "If *you* don't make it into the choir, getting along will be the easiest thing in the world," I said, a bit surprised at how sarcastic my words sounded. Or how easy it was to say them.

"I'm *in*—the choir, that is," she announced with way too much pride.

"How do you know? Auditions aren't till Tuesday."

"Mr. Keller wants *me* no matter what. If there are too many sopranos, he'll use me as an accompanist at the piano." Downright haughty, that's how she sounded. "Uh, excuse me, Holly. Jared's calling. They're bringing a tray up from the cafeteria for me. I've got a dinner date with You-Know-Who. Bye."

Andie's words stung. Hanging up the phone, I stumbled back to my room. I fell into bed and stared at the underside of my canopy, feeling terribly cheated. My best friend had trespassed on *my* territory. *On my heart.*

I don't know how long I stared at the canopy, but soon I had the urge to grab Bearie-O and throw him across the room. I didn't need him reminding me of Andie. Not anymore. So I tossed him off my bed.

Mom called me downstairs to play caroms with her and Carrie. I played even though I didn't feel like it. "Please, will you take me to see Jared?" I begged Mom when Carrie's turn came around.

Then, when it was Mom's turn, she placed the white shooter on the board, aimed, and shot. "I don't know the family very well," she said.

"Why couldn't you get to know Mrs. Wilkins?" I pleaded as two of my green caroms slid into a side pocket. "Please, Mom?"

It took three more turns and saying "please" at least five more times before Mom even considered taking me. Finally, after I talked about how the Wilkins family attended our church, Jared was in the youth group, and on and on, she agreed to drive to the hospital on the way to church.

"We'll stop there briefly," Mom said.

Briefly, momentarily . . . whatever. I was beyond thrilled.

♥   ♥   ♥

Dressel Hills Hospital was small but well decorated. Cozy mauve couches and chairs were scattered around the waiting area. Potted palms and spider plants gave it a comfortable feeling. Oil paintings of local spots—mountains, waterfalls, and meadows—were spotlighted on the wall.

Mom asked for Jared's room number at the receptionist's desk. As we walked down a long, narrow hall, I became more nervous with every step. What would I say to Jared? Would Andie still be hanging around?

We rounded a corner, and I spotted Mrs. Wilkins chatting with Andie's mother in the waiting area near room 204—Jared's. So Andie *was* here. Mom shot me a glance. I nodded and pointed back at her. I wanted *her* to make the necessary introductions.

Somehow, I don't know how, I managed to smile and shake hands with Mrs. Wilkins, a small woman with blue eyes and a smile just like Jared's. "Why don't you go on in and see Jared?" she said. "Andie's with him."

"Are you sure it's all right?" I asked.

"Well, to tell the truth, he might already be sleeping," Mrs. Wilkins said. "He just had some morphine for pain."

Jared in pain? My heart jumped. I wandered over to his room.

Pausing at the doorway, I spied Andie. She sat curled up in a chair, close to Jared's hospital bed, like she was monitoring his every breath. He was propped up with a zillion pillows, his right leg supported by a pulley system above the bed.

Andie looked up at that moment. "Holly!" she said in her most charming voice. "Come right in."

I approached the bed just as Jared let out a tiny, high-pitched snort. He was snoring.

Andie began to explain. "He's had morphine for pain."

"I know. His mom already told me." I found another chair and pulled it over next to Andie's and sat down. A long silence settled over the room. I was boiling inside.

At last, I blurted out what I was thinking. I just couldn't hold in my thoughts any longer. "Look, Andie," I said, leaning toward her. "Jared likes *me*, I know he does."

She crossed her chubby little legs. "Maybe he did once, but this is *now*," she said. "Whatever you had, or thought you had, well, it's over. You're history."

This was beyond my worst nightmare! Jared interested in Andie? He had said he liked tall, skinny girls. Andie was anything but that.

"I know you're wrong," I argued. "You must've been dreaming—wishing it were true—when you thought he touched your hand."

"Do you want a written statement?" She leaned closer to Jared, her eyes scanning the rings and pulleys that held his fractured leg in place. "He wants me to watch over him while he sleeps."

"Oh, puh-lease." I rolled my eyes. "He doesn't need mothering, Andie. He's got a real mother for that." Then I lit into her. "You're the poorest excuse I know for a best friend."

"What about you? You didn't back away when you knew how much I liked him, did you?"

"That's different," I managed to say. "He was the first boy to accept me as I am."

"You mean skin and bones?"

A low blow! Something snapped inside me. "That's it," I shouted. "You'll never see our Loyalty Papers again."

"Whatever!" She fluffed her dark locks. "You don't know what you're saying. Your life's a big, fat zero without me."

"That's what you think," I growled. "Why don't *you* go home and leave me alone with Jared?"

"If I'm not here when he wakes up—well, I just don't know what he'd do. We have a very special bond," she said in her sickening-sweet voice.

"Well, he must be desperate, then. Just pack up your precious keyboard and get out of here."

Mom and Mrs. Wilkins poked their heads in the doorway. Mom looked puzzled. "Is everything all right?"

"Not really," I said. "Andie was just leaving."

Mom caught on quickly. "Girls, can you solve your problems elsewhere?" Then she motioned to me. I got up reluctantly and started toward her.

Jared woke up. "I . . . I heard voices," he said.

Andie jumped up to reassure him. "It was nothing. Nothing at all."

Jared's father came in, carrying a white Styrofoam cup brimming with hot coffee. He was good-looking, too, with blond hair and a mustache. He pulled a chair over next to the bed. "Thanks, girls, for dropping by to visit our son," he said.

"Girls?" Jared said sleepily. "Where?"

Mom's firm touch on my arm signaled the end of my visit. "It was nice to meet you," she said to Jared's parents.

"We'll be sure to mention Jared during the prayer requests at the service tonight."

We smiled and shook hands all around. Then I headed down the hall with my family. Carrie held Mom's hand, and I moped behind. I felt like picking a fight. With Andie, with Mom—with anyone in sight.

"What's come over you?" Mom asked as we drove to church in the snowy stillness.

I shrugged. "You wouldn't understand."

"Holly?" she said in her warning voice, which meant, *You'd better shape up—or else.*

"Don't you remember?" I said. "It's all part of becoming a young woman. Isn't that what you said?"

"I've never seen you so rude."

"For as long as I live, I never want to see Andrea Martinez again," I announced as we pulled into the parking lot of the church. "Never!"

♥ ♥ ♥

Later, when we arrived at home after the short service, a strange sense of delight swept over me as I slammed the car door and stomped into the house. Like an arrow, I darted straight to my room. There, I pulled the Loyalty Papers from the special folder. I looked at them—fondly for a moment—then I began to rip each page in two. I scattered the pieces all over the floor. Finally I slam-dunked Bearie-O into the trash can, head first.

This was it. My friendship with Andrea Martinez was over!

Tuesday afternoon—choir auditions! To sing with a traveling group had always been one of my dreams. But as I sat waiting in the hallway leading to the choir room at church, I wasn't so sure my dream was going to come true. The place was crammed with guys and girls. They lined the hallway, leaning against the plaque-covered wall. They sat cross-legged on the floor, each reviewing last-minute dynamics and phrasing.

Mom and I were together. She sat calmly waiting for my audition while she read a novel. Me? I pulled and twisted my long hair.

"We've practiced over twenty times," I told Alissa Morgan, the girl ahead of me, when she asked.

"That's probably a good idea by the looks of things." She stood on her tiptoes, searching for someone.

"Are all these kids in the church youth group?" I asked.

"Yep." She spotted her friend and called, "Hey, Danny, over here."

A tan-faced boy with reddish hair bounded over to us.

"How's it going in there?" Alissa's head bobbed toward the auditioning room.

"Fierce competition," Danny Myers said. "How are *you* doing? Nervous?" He touched her shoulder.

"I'll be glad when this day's over," she admitted.

"Hey, relax, you'll make it." Then, spying me, he said, "I remember you. Holly Meredith, right?"

I nodded.

"Your mom makes the best cookies ever. Snickersomething."

I smiled. "That's close. They're snickerdoodles, and they're *my* favorite, too."

He nodded. "She brought some to our Christmas bake sale. That's when I first met you and your sister. You two look so much alike."

"The tall and the short of it," I replied.

"How tall are you, anyway?" Alissa asked.

"Almost five-eight." I beamed down at her.

Danny grinned. "One more inch, and you'll catch me." He had a comfortable way about him.

"Wanna get some water before you try out?" he asked Alissa.

"Good idea. My throat's so dry," she said. Danny walked with her down the hall to the water fountain.

I sighed. *Some day, a boy will treat me like that.*

♥   ♥   ♥

Thirty minutes dragged by. A heaviness hung in the air. One girl came out of the choir room in tears. Next came a boy, smiling. He jumped up and down all the way to the end of the hallway, exclaiming, "Yes . . . so cool!"

"*He's* confident," Mom said, looking up from her book.

An older girl poked her head out the choir room. "Holly Meredith, you're next."

With as much courage as possible, I entered the choir room. I did fine on the sightsinging and my prepared piece . . . but the arpeggios. Gulp!

On the way home, Mom chattered with excitement. "You sang like an angel, Holly-Heart."

Maybe she thought so, but I knew better.

When I wrote the heading in my journal for the day it was: "Tuesday—An Alto's Nightmare. But I survived it." It was the only mention I made of my pitiful audition. The rest of the diary entry was taken up with how sweetly Danny Myers treated Alissa Morgan. I couldn't remember seeing them together before. But it wasn't any surprise, because I hadn't started attending youth group. Not yet.

To be honest, it felt weird going this long without talking to Andie. I pulled Bearie-O out of the trash and told *him* all about my audition. He was a good listener. Never talked back. Never threw junk out of his locker, making piles in the hall. Never stole boyfriends. Or called me stupid nicknames, like Heartless. Even though he really belonged to Andie, after six years I thought of him as mine. I had a right to.

♥　♥　♥

Wednesday morning arrived. Eighteen days to thrilling thirteen! I wrote the number on my bulletin board. The days were crawling by like snails.

Before Mom left for work, I asked her about my party. "Can we plan it tonight?"

"After school."

"Perfect," I said, chewing on the ends of my hair.

"You'll split your ends," Mom said.

I wanted to say *who cares?* but bit my tongue.

That afternoon following gym class Andie bragged about Jared's musical genius to the girls in the locker room. The only good thing about gym today was Miss Neff didn't call me "Holly-Bones." A first.

Maybe she noticed some development that I missed, I thought, standing sideways at the mirror.

My hair was still damp from a quick shower when I reached for my history book and slammed my locker. Racing toward history class, I accidentally bumped into Danny Myers in the hallway.

"Oh, excuse me," I said as he bent down and helped me pick up my books.

"Holly Meredith, right? Five-eight? Look-a-like little sis? Bookworm mother, right? Favorite cookie—snicker-doodles?"

"You're a walking, breathing computer chip, right?"

He stopped, took a long look at me, and smiled. "That's my specialty—memory. I work at it."

I straightened my books. "It shows."

"See you at youth group next Tuesday?"

"When I'm thirteen I'll start going. About a month to go."

"Really?" There was that smile. "They should change those rules." And he was off in the opposite direction.

For a nanosecond I actually forgot about Jared Wilkins.

♥   ♥   ♥

In history class, I doodled on my notebook. How long before my letter to Daddy arrived at his home in California? I had mailed it on the way to school this morning. Mom was still in the dark about what I'd decided, of course. Best that way.

The teacher droned on about the decisive battle in the Norman conquest of England. And I daydreamed through class. I figured I could catch up by reading the account of the skirmish tonight.

After history, I caught up with Billy Hill heading for his locker. "Wait up," I called.

"Hey," he said, smiling.

"Any news about Jared?" I asked.

"He had his surgery Monday night. They put a rod in his tibia bone."

"Which one's that?"

He pointed to his own leg. "Shinbone."

"Is he in a cast yet?"

He nodded.

"For how long?"

"About six weeks. Bummer, huh?"

"So he'll get the cast off by spring break?"

He scratched his head. "Yeah, it should be off by then." He looked serious. "The worst thing about this whole mess is it should never have happened."

"What do you mean?"

He glanced up the hallway, like he had to check out the turf. "Several guys were spotting Jared on the tramp before he fell. One of them was Tom Sly. When Jared began to lose balance, Tom backed away. On purpose."

This was rotten. I could hardly believe it.

But there was more. "Jared and Tom had been hassling

each other a lot during practice games after school lately."

"So . . . do you think Tom wanted Jared to get hurt?"

"Who knows." He ran his fingers through his hair. "Thing is, there was major hostility between them. You heard about the smoking thing Tom tried to pull on Jared and me, didn't you?"

I nodded. "Too weird."

I stopped with Billy at his locker. There was a note taped to the outside. "Looks like a note from the coach," he said.

I peered over his shoulder as he read it. "Late practice?"

"Yeah. Things are real tough without Jared around. The team needs him."

"Looks like Tom's revenge is messing things up for all of you."

"No kidding." He closed his locker. "You like Jared, don't you?" He looked me square in the face.

I felt my cheeks starting to warm up.

"You're blushing," he said with a smile.

"Gotta run," I said, heading for my next class.

In English, I jotted down seven names on a note pad. These kids were going to receive invitations to my thirteenth birthday bash. Andie was *not* on the list.

Jared was.

12

The back door slammed behind me as I came into the house. Dropping my book bag on the bar in the kitchen, I heard Carrie calling to me from the family room. "Jared called."

My hand froze as I unzipped my jacket. Jared! My heart pounded. I went to the top of the stairs and tried to sound casual. "When did he call?"

She came skipping up the stairway and watched as I hung my jacket in the hall closet. "He called right after school was out," she said. "He wants you to call him back."

"Thanks for the message." I picked up my book bag. Slowly, I headed toward the steps leading to my bedroom, then raced to the phone in Mom's room so Carrie wouldn't see or hear me.

"Room 204, please," I told the hospital operator when she answered.

Butterflies flittered in my stomach as I waited.

"Wilkins' Torture Chamber," a male voice said.

"Is that you, Jared?"

"Who else?" He was laughing.

"It's Holly."

"I'd know your voice anywhere." He paused. "How's school?"

"Okay, I guess. The team misses you. Everyone does," I said, thinking I was the one who missed him most. "I visited you Sunday afternoon, but you were snoring."

He chuckled. "Morphine knocked me out a couple days before surgery. But Doc says I'm going home tomorrow."

"Really?" I was dying to see him again.

"How'd your audition go?"

"Let's just say I've sung better," I told him.

"Hope you make it." His voice was soft. "Choir tour wouldn't be the same without *you*, Holly-Heart."

My heart flip-flopped. "Mr. Keller's going to post the list this weekend. But you already know you made it. They need guys in choir . . . I heard that before auditions." Fidgeting, I folded my long hair over the top of my head. It hung down like a satiny curtain in front of me. "I might be going to visit my dad in California for spring break," I said.

"You can't do that . . . it's the choir tour."

"But isn't the tour this *summer?*"

"No, it's during spring break, and we're going to Disneyland."

"Guess I'll just have to visit my dad another time," I said, wondering how I could've gotten so mixed up.

Jared changed the subject. "Don't we have a skiing date this weekend?"

"With your leg in a cast?" Some comedian.

"And why not?" Jared asked, flirting.

"But your leg . . ."

"No, really." He sounded more serious now. "I'll be home from the hospital on Friday, and the youth group's going tobogganing Saturday at Jake's Run. How about going along to keep me company at the lodge?"

Jake's Run—the steepest, wildest toboggan ride this side of the Continental Divide. It had a cozy, A-frame lodge with a coffee shop and a lounge with a huge stone fireplace. "How can you get around with your leg in a cast?" I asked.

"I've got crutches now. And my folks think it would be good for me to get out, as long as I'm careful. What do you say?"

As much as I wanted to go along, Mom would never agree. She always said I had to be much older—like in my twenties—and oozing with responsibility before I could even think of dating. Besides, I wasn't old enough to go on the youth group activities yet, according to the youth pastor. I sighed. "I don't think I can," I said. "Sorry."

"Why not?"

I dodged the question. I still had plenty of doubts about Jared, and they confused me. What really had happened between Jared and Andie at the hospital? Had she lied about his wanting her there? Eating supper at the hospital? All of it bugged me. "Isn't Andie going on the ski trip?" I asked.

"I don't know," he said. "Why?"

"I thought you liked Andie. *She* thinks you do."

"Andie and I are just friends," he protested.

Carrie was suddenly standing in front of me. She was tugging at my shirt, even though I shooed her away. Her eyes were demanding little specks, growing wider with every second.

"Look, I've gotta go. My little sister needs me."

"I'll call you tomorrow," Jared said. "Bye, Holly."

I held the phone in my hand, reluctant to hang up.

Turning to Carrie, I said, "Please don't ever do that again. This phone call was private."

"So that's why you came up here—to Mom's bedroom—to talk." Her childishness was annoying. "You were hiding from me."

"You'll understand some day."

"So you must *really* like the Jared person," she taunted.

"You'll never know." I raced her downstairs to the kitchen, where we helped ourselves to carrots and dip.

If what Carrie said just now was true, why did I feel both happy and miserable?

♥ ♥ ♥

The next two days in school dragged on. Jared called Thursday night and pleaded with me to go to Jake's Run with the youth group. I told him I hadn't asked my mom yet.

Before I knew it, Saturday had arrived. Sleep-in time!

Mom jostled me out of my covers. "Wake up, Holly-Heart. This is the day we've been waiting for. The choir list will be posted at church." She tossed Bearie-O at me.

I kicked my leg over the side of the bed. Slowly easing out, I stood and stared at the mirror. Was this the face of a traveling singer? A new youth choir member?

Right after breakfast the phone rang. It was Andie.

"I'm not sure I want to talk to you," I said.

"Listen, something's really crazy," she said. "It's just too awful."

"Why are you calling me? We're not talking, remember?"

"It's such a shame," she said, ignoring me. "It really is."

"*What* is?" I asked.

"Holly, I'll try to break this to you gently."

"Break what to me?"

"You asked for it," she said. "Your name's nowhere to be seen on the list for choir."

I slammed down the phone. Enough of her gloating. Mr. Keller and his precious choir could go sing in their sleep for all I cared.

Determined to ignore Andie and her nasty news, I marched to the garage. There, I found a box of lawn and leaf trash bags. I scribbled a note to Andie, pinned it to Bearie-O, and stuffed him inside.

"I'm going for a walk, Mom." I yanked my jacket and gloves out of the closet.

"Where on earth are you headed in this cold?" she called.

I slung the trash bag over my shoulder. "I won't be long, I promise."

Trudging down the sidewalk—where Andie and I had played the don't-step-on-a-crack-or-you'll-break-your-mother's-back game when we were kids—I headed off to Andie's house, only a few blocks away.

When I arrived, I noticed the mail carrier coming up the street. Perfect! In a few minutes the deed would be done. I hid behind a clump of aspen trees in front of her house till the mail truck passed by. Then, in a flash, I dashed to Andie's mailbox, opened it, and shoved the trash bag inside—Bearie-O and all.

♥ ♥ ♥

Back home, I told Mom to forget about checking on the choir list at church.

"Why's that, honey?" she said, looking up from the dining room table, where she was writing a list.

I tossed my mittens up onto the shelf in the hall closet. "I already know I wasn't picked for choir. But it's okay—I didn't want to see Andie's fat little face every day of my life during spring break anyway."

"What's going on between you two?" Mom asked, putting her pen down and staring at me.

"We're through, she and I. Finished. The final end of us has come." Then, on the heels of that, I made the cold announcement about Daddy. "Oh, by the way, I thought you might like to know . . . I've decided to visit Daddy during spring break."

She looked positively shocked. "Isn't this a bit sudden?"

"I'm sick of being around here. I'm sick of everything!" I sat down on the floor in a heap.

"Holly-Heart, you're terribly upset about the choir tour, aren't you?" She left her list behind and sat on the floor beside me, stroking my hair.

"It's that, and everything else. You . . . you just don't understand anymore."

"We can talk about it."

"It's too late. My letter to Daddy has probably arrived there by now."

"We could've discussed this. I wish you'd talked to me first."

I looked at her. "Well, Daddy must think I'm old enough to decide where I want to spend my vacations." With that, I got up and trudged upstairs. At the top, I turned to see Mom, still sitting on the floor, looking terribly sad.

In my room, I tried to think of five exceptionally creative ways to ask Mom about going tobogganing with the youth group. But after letting some time pass, and then going back downstairs to talk to her, the only thing I came up with was this: "May I please go to Jake's Run with the youth group this afternoon?"

She was sitting at the dining room table, now clipping coupons. She looked up, scissors in hand. "It's a little short notice, don't you think?" *Snip* went her scissors.

"I guess, but I just found out about it," I said as politely as a charm-school graduate.

"From whom?" She added three more coupons to her pile.

Somehow I knew *that* was coming.

"Jared Wilkins told me," I said.

"Didn't he just get out of the hospital?" There was no fooling her.

"Yes, but he needs some company, some fresh air, too." I pleaded my case upside and down. Mom was a hard one to crack.

"Your friend Jared wouldn't be foolish enough to go tobogganing with his leg in a cast, would he?"

"Oh, Mom. Be fair. We won't be outside. He and I will probably talk inside the lodge . . . wait while the others go sledding, you know."

"What you just described sounds much too exclusive. Besides, the whole idea of going with a group is to be *with* the group."

"But I've been alone with Jared before. We went to the Soda Straw and . . ."

Oops. What had made me mention that?

Mom's eyes got all squinty and she said, slowly and evenly, "You did *what?*"

"We just had a Coke one day after school, and Andie came by anyway, so it wasn't all so bad. I'm responsible. Please, Mom? Please may I go?"

"Not this time, Holly-Heart," she said flatly.

That nickname meant I was loved, but I certainly didn't feel like it, at least not now. "I wish you wouldn't call me that," I said over my shoulder as I stomped up the steps, thinking of ways to escape for the afternoon.

Five minutes alone in my room was all the time it took. When Mom was ready to go grocery shopping, I'd say I had to finish up some homework. Then when the house was empty I'd hop a bus to the church. The perfect plan!

After lunch I volunteered to clean up the kitchen. Mom seemed to be impressed. Carrie was obviously relieved.

By the time Mom was ready to do the shopping, I had convinced her to let me stay home to do a report for school. And the cool thing was she fell for it.

House empty, I slipped into my soft pink turtleneck sweater and brushed my hair. My heart pounded with the daring adventure ahead.

♥　　♥　　♥

The lodge above Jake's Run buzzed with noise as skiers clumped in their boots across the wooden floor to the snack bar. Jackets hung on pegs, their bright colors splashed against the dark paneling.

Jared and I went through the snack bar to a quieter spot, a small room with cozy sofas and tall windows over-looking the slopes. A roaring fire crackled in a white-brick fireplace nearby. I warmed my feet as Jared showed off his storytelling abilities to the perfect audience: me.

"That's fabulous," I said when he finished. "You should write some of them down."

"Sometimes I do. But mostly they're in my head. What about you?"

"I'd write all the time, if I could."

"I think we're made for each other," he said.

I laughed, enjoying the attention. Too much. "What do you mean . . . just because we both like to write?"

"That's one of the cool things about you, Holly. You don't play games. You're honest."

I took a deep breath. He sure wouldn't be saying that if he knew how I'd lied to get out of the house.

Later, I signed his cast. In red letters, I wrote, LOVE, HOLLY. Our hands touched.

"Does this mean we're, uh, you know . . . going to-gether?" he asked, propping a pillow under his bad leg.

I ignored the question. "Here, let me help you."

"Well, Holly-Heart?" He'd called me by my nickname again.

I blushed. "Okay."

Jared's eyes twinkled. "Fabulous," he said softly, using *my* word.

We played six games of checkers while the youth group tobogganed. What a great time I was having. If it hadn't been Jared smiling and flirting across the checker board at me, I would have been totally miserable.

By the time the sun's rays disappeared behind the

mountains, around the supper hour, I knew that Mom would know the truth.

All the way home Jared held my hand. He said I was perfect. Tall and skinny . . . so what?

I believed him. This was a first crush at its very best. Well, almost. The guilt from lying and sneaking off grew more powerful as each snow-packed mile crunched under our bus.

Then, on the final mountain pass, the bus broke down. Danny and Alissa and several others got out as the driver surveyed the problem. I watched Alissa from inside the bus. She looked like a snow princess; her face glowed—half windburn, part sunburn, and a little adoration for Danny Myers thrown in.

I checked my watch. Mom would be worried sick by now. But when Jared winked at me, my heart flip-flopped and I pushed my worries away.

♥ ♥ ♥

Three hours and a growling stomach later, I turned my house key in the lock. Carrie caught me tiptoeing in. "Mom, she's home," she shouted, throwing her arms around me.

Mom eyeballed me from the sofa, closing the book she was reading. Slowly, she stood up. Her precise movements spelled trouble. "You've been gone a long time, Holly-Heart." It was a statement, not a question.

She knew.

"I won't lie to you anymore, Mom. I went with the youth group to Jake's Run."

She squinted her eyes. "It was deceitful, Holly, and willfully disobedient. You're grounded. No friends, no TV, and no phone for a full week."

"That long?" I cried.

"There are leftovers in the fridge. Eat something before you go to bed. I'll have a list of chores on the table in the morning."

"But, Mom, I—"

"No back talk or I'll add more." She turned toward the kitchen. I'd never seen Mom this rattled before.

"She forgets how it feels to be a kid." I let the words softly slip from my lips.

"I'm gonna tell," Carrie said.

"Who cares?" I shot back, taking the steps two at a time.

Safe in my room, I wrote a heading for today's journal entry—"My perfect afternoon with Jared Wilkins." Paying for my deceit with a week's grounding was even trade for the hours I'd spent with the cutest, sweetest boy ever.

13

The first week of February —seven days of pure boredom! Going to school was what I lived for. Jared was back at school, and I was his faithful helper—carrying his tray at lunch, sharpening pencils in class, and helping with his crutches in the hall and everywhere else.

Andie was furious, following us around. But Jared was polite even though it was obvious she couldn't accept the facts. Jared was mine now.

After-school hours dragged endlessly. Even Bearie-O was unavailable for dumping my woes. And when Corky, my old teddy bear, showed up on our porch on Tuesday with a note pinned to *his* ear, I knew my friendship with Andie was in deep trouble. But I didn't care.

Finally the week of being grounded was over. Freedom! Talking on the phone was pure heaven. Best of all, my birthday was getting closer. Mom stocked up on four flavors of ice cream for the birthday bash. One of the flavors was bubble gum, with delicious pieces of pink gum scattered in. And ten toppings! I couldn't wait for the best ice-cream party ever.

On Sunday afternoon I did fancy cuttings with lavender

and blue crepe paper. Everything was set for my party the following Saturday.

Then on the Thursday before my birthday, I came home to find a note propped against the cookie jar. *Holly: Carrie and I are at the travel agency. We'll be back soon. Love, Mom.*

I poured a tall glass of milk, stirred chocolate syrup in, and grabbed two cookies to nibble on. My imagination ran wild.

Just great, I thought. *She's planning some exotic travel adventure during spring break while I'm in California visiting Daddy. . . .*

While pigging out on cookies, I began to compose a romantic note to Jared. I was half finished when the garage door rumbled open. Quickly, I hid the perfumed stationery.

Carrie ran into the kitchen out of breath. "We got plane tickets, and Mom has something to tell you."

Was it Paris or the Orient?

Mom walked in at a snail's pace, her face drawn. She pulled out a kitchen chair and sat down. I didn't want to look at her. *This is some cruel trick,* I thought. *Did she really think I'd cancel my plans to go with them instead?*

"Holly-Heart." She breathed a heavy sigh. "Aunt Marla died this morning."

I was stunned.

"We're flying to Pennsylvania tomorrow."

Carrie asked, "Do we have to wear black to the funeral?"

"No, darling," Mom said, pulling her near.

Tears began to trickle down my cheeks. I couldn't help myself.

"Your aunt's pain is finally over," she said, holding out

her arms to me. "She's with Jesus now."

"But . . . what about Holly's party?" Carrie asked, rubbing her eyes.

"I'm sorry, dear, we'll have to postpone it," she said, picking up Goofey and petting him.

I pulled on my hair. "Who feels like celebrating, anyway? I'll let everyone know."

The timing was terrible. I'd never anticipated the possibility of a funeral disrupting my thirteenth birthday party plans. Worst of all, Aunt Marla was dead.

♥   ♥   ♥

Grandpa and Grandma Meredith met us with hugs and tears at the airport. They drove us through the narrow tree-lined streets to their house. Quietly unpacking, I thought back to the happiest times in this house. When Mom and Daddy were still married, we came for week-long visits here in the summer. Uncle Jack and Aunt Marla and our cousins drove the short distance to Grandpa's house on the Fourth of July. We kids would make short order of the corn on the cob until Grandpa teased that we might turn into walking ears of corn ourselves. At dusk, we wrote our names in the air with the sparklers Uncle Jack gave us. Daddy and his sister, Aunt Marla, would kiss and hug good-bye. Very sweet.

I swallowed hard, fighting back the tears. Those days were forever past, not just because Aunt Marla was gone, but because Daddy was, too.

Carrie came in and sat on the quilted bedspread. "Mommy says our dad will be at the funeral tomorrow. Do you think he'll bring his new wife and kid?" Carrie asked.

"Maybe," I said, brushing her hair. "I wonder if he'll recognize us." I felt giddy with excitement and sadness all mixed together.

"We sent him school pictures last fall, so he should."

I stopped brushing. "Oh yeah, and mine looked pathetic because I couldn't get my hair to do anything," I said, staring at the mirror. My hair looked droopy now, too. Humidity was a big problem. Even in the winter, Pennsylvania air was heavy with moisture.

The funeral was on Saturday—the day my ice-cream party had been scheduled. The church foyer was crowded when we arrived. People lined up to sign a formal-looking white book on a small table encircled with red roses. Mothers with young children and their executive-type husbands—probably men who worked with Uncle Jack— waited to say their good-byes to Aunt Marla.

The family was supposed to gather in a small reception room behind the church sanctuary. Carrie and I followed Mom down the long hallway to the private room. Grandma and Grandpa were sitting with Uncle Jack and the cousins. We settled into the soft chairs behind them.

Relatives I hardly knew stood around. Mom introduced Carrie and me to them; they were from Daddy's side of the family.

Behind me I heard whispering and turned to see who it was. In the doorway stood a handsome man wearing a navy blue suit. He was with a smartly dressed woman.

Four years of mounting curiosity hit me in the face. This man was my father.

"Holly?" he said. "What a beauty you are." He turned

to the woman. "Honey, I want you to meet my daughter Holly."

"Hello," I said, suddenly shy. I reached out to touch her gloved hand.

"Holly, I'd like you to meet Saundra, my wife."

By then Carrie was tugging at me to leave. I grabbed her arm and turned her around.

"Well, hello there, Carrie," Daddy said, bending low.

She looked up at me, confused. "That's him?" she whispered back at me.

Daddy smiled. "It's wonderful to see both of you."

Saundra said, "We were happy to receive your letter, Holly."

"Yes," Daddy said. "I was planning to call . . . to set up a flight schedule. But now we can discuss the trip in person." He stepped toward me like he wanted to hug me, so I offered a quick one.

"I'll see you at the dinner for the family tonight," I said, turning to look for Carrie.

She was standing across the room beside our young cousin Stephanie, who sat, eyes swollen, leaning against Mom. It was time for Aunt Marla's funeral to begin.

The church was filled with a sweet fragrance from the many floral sprays. The organ played softly, and voices were hushed. I touched the tissues in my dress pocket. I knew I'd need them.

♥   ♥   ♥

After the funeral, we waited to ride in one of the black

limousines to the cemetery. Carrie begged Mom to let Stephie ride with us.

"Uncle Jack wants all of the children to ride together," Mom told us as we walked down the church steps.

The limo pulled up, but there was only room for two more people.

"I'll ride in the next one," I said. Mom agreed.

Another limo came around, and I got in. Daddy and his new wife climbed in behind me. He looked lousy from grief; his face was pale and his eyes were red.

I felt numb. Aunt Marla's funeral wasn't exactly the best place to reunite with my long-lost father.

The ride to the cemetery was awkward. Here I sat across from this Saundra person trying to be polite when I really wanted to shout: Leave me alone with my dad!

What was she doing here, anyway? She'd probably never even met Aunt Marla. To top things off, she began chattering about spring break and where we could go sightseeing. Stuff like that. "We've planned a delightful time for you," she said. "Next month, isn't it?" She opened her purse, took out lipstick and a mirror, and began to touch up her already bright red lips.

"The last week in March." I glanced at Daddy. "Maybe you should talk to Mom about it."

"There will be plenty of time for that tonight," he said, adjusting his striped tie. He was as handsome as I'd remembered. "Tomorrow is your birthday," he commented. "When are you flying back?"

"We'll get home late tomorrow night." Too late to have the ice-cream party. Too late to celebrate my milestone birthday with my friends. With Jared.

Saundra asked, "Is there something special you'd like for your big day?"

I tugged on my hair as I thought of the most special things in all the world. They couldn't be purchased by her or anyone. But there was *something*. "The latest mystery novel by Marty Leigh just came out. I'd like that."

Saundra smiled, closing her compact mirror with a click. Did she really think she could make points with me so easily?

"How are you doing in school?" Daddy asked. "Good grades? Lots of friends?"

I told him about my B+ average, but I didn't tell him about my ongoing journal writing or about Jared.

♥　♥　♥

At supper, Stephie sat with Carrie and me. Her nose was red from too much blowing, but her eyes looked less swollen now. When the caterer came around to get our beverage orders, Stephie ordered a soda, then looked at her dad to see if he would disapprove. Uncle Jack didn't say a word. His usual fun-loving smile seemed to have disappeared.

"Mom would never let me drink pop at meals," Stephie whispered to us. "Things are going to be different without her."

I nearly choked on my ice water. I couldn't imagine being eight years old and motherless.

"Things changed at our house when Daddy left, but not that much," Carrie spoke up. I wondered if she truly remembered.

After the lemon angel food cake was served for dessert, Grandpa signaled for everyone's attention. "My grand-daughter Holly will be celebrating her thirteenth birthday tomorrow. Please join me in singing the birthday song."

He motioned for me to stand while they sang. Relatives I'd never met and friends of Uncle Jack's sang "Happy Birthday to You" with amazing gusto. I glanced at Daddy. He winked at me. Mom, at the other end of the long table, beamed with pride. Some birthday party! I should have been eating ice cream with Jared right about now.

Suddenly I felt ashamed. Aunt Marla was gone, and all I could think about was missing a boy. What was wrong with me? What was I thinking?

Late that night, lying awake in Grandpa's big house, I stared at the shadows dancing eerily on the ceiling. In a few minutes I'd be a teenager. "Dear Lord," I prayed, "let this be my magical night." He knew what I meant.

The next morning I woke with a jolt. A small backbone pressed against me. It was Carrie's. I lay still in the quiet. The table clock's ticking soothed me. Today was Valentine's Day. My day.

Uncle Jack and our cousins came over for breakfast. The boys wolfed down their pancakes, and Uncle Jack said, "Slow down, fellas." Usually he would have made a joke of the boys gobbling down their food like so many turkeys, or something like that.

I remembered why we'd called them stair-step cousins. Sitting across from them was like looking at a descending scale. Stan first, then Phil, then Mark. Little Stephanie last.

Grandpa came downstairs carrying a box wrapped in bright pink-and-red paper. He planted a wet kiss on my cheek. "Happy birthday, Holly-Heart."

Inside, a huge white teddy bear stared up at me. Grandma had cross-stitched a red heart on him, and a ten-dollar bill shaped like a bow tie was pinned under his chin.

"Thanks." I hugged the bear first, then Grandpa and Grandma.

"What's his name?" Stephie asked.

"I'll have to think about it first. Let's see what kind of personality he has." I pulled out my chair for Grandpa. "How did you know what I wanted?"

"A little bird flew around and chirped it in this ear." He pulled on his left ear.

"Oh, Grandpa," Carrie said. "You're just teasing."

A few minutes later, the doorbell rang. Grandma hurried to the living room.

"Happy birthday, Holly." It was Daddy—and his new wife.

"Come in," I said shyly, inching toward them.

Daddy pulled an envelope out of his pocket. It was a gift certificate to a national chain of bookstores. "You can get that mystery book you wanted and many more," he said with a grin.

"You should be able to buy an entire month's worth," Saundra said, smiling too broadly.

"Thanks, this is fabulous." The words choked in my throat.

Carrie lost interest quickly and disappeared upstairs with the cousins. Mom hadn't ventured into the living room. I could see her alone in the kitchen, clearing things away.

"We really can't stay," Daddy said. "We have to catch a plane, but we'll be in touch."

Uncle Jack held out his hand. "Good to see you again."

But Daddy ignored my uncle's hand, hugging him instead. "Take care of those kids, Jack," he said, a twinge of longing in his voice.

Grandma kissed him and said to call when they arrived home.

"Take it easy, son," Grandpa said. His eyes glistened.

"I'll have my travel agent line up a flight for you soon," Daddy said to me. I reached for him. He held me. And then, they were both gone.

After Daddy and Saundra left, the rest of us headed off to Sunday school and church. All but Uncle Jack. He said he needed some time alone. I wished I could say something to make him feel better, but what could I say or do? His beloved wife had died, leaving him and the children alone. As we headed out the door, I hurried over to him and gave him a big hug. He hugged me back and kissed me on the forehead. "You're sweet, Holly," he whispered.

During church, we sat toward the back of the sanctuary, passing tissues up and down the row during worship. Why did such joyful songs now seem so terribly sad? I kept praying: *Dear God, be with Uncle Jack and my cousins. Please comfort them.*

When church was over and we were back at my grandparents' house, I retreated to the room where I'd slept. Silently, I closed the door. It was time to pour out my feelings on paper. Rummaging through my suitcase, I located my journal. In honor of my dear aunt Marla, I wrote her birthdate and death date in my diary. I stared at what I'd written till the tears came. She was too young to die—just two years older than Mom!

♥   ♥   ♥

Our flight home was long and boring. When we arrived home, Mom set the suitcases on the kitchen floor and promptly marched Carrie off to bed. I went up to my room and read my Bible until my eyes drooped. They felt like Bearie-O's eyes had looked. I missed him *and* his owner, my former best friend. But I didn't miss Andie's disgusting attention-getting routines. No way.

I hugged my new birthday bear to me and thought of Jared. It had been three whole days since I'd seen him— the longest ever. I couldn't wait to see him again. Turning thirteen was perfect with him as my friend!

The next day at school I told everyone on the list about the *new* date for the party: Saturday, February 20. Everyone but Jared. I couldn't find him. Not in the library. Not at his locker between classes.

At last, I saw him in the cafeteria at lunch . . . with Andie! She was getting some grated cheese for his spaghetti. I waited in the hot-lunch line, seething, as she slid into the seat next to him, shaking the cheese on his plate.

I felt like hanging her upside down by her fat little toes.

Billy Hill slipped in line behind me. "Looks like Andie's earning points with Jared," he said. "The second you left for Pennsylvania, she moved in."

"She did?" I was crushed.

"Andie didn't waste any time—helping with his crutches, running errands . . . you name it."

I stared at the two of them. They looked so cozy over there, talking and laughing. I set my tray down on the table, seething with anger.

Billy looked at me. "Hey, you okay?"

I blew my breath out hard. "Jared's a two-timing jerk."

"Funny. Andie doesn't seem to mind," Billy said.

I sat down with my spaghetti. "How could he do this to me?" I said between bites.

Danny and Alissa came into the cafeteria together. They sat at the end of our table. Before they ate, they bowed their heads for grace.

Billy glanced at them, frowned, then got up to leave. "See you around, Holly. Hang in there, okay?"

I moved over across from Danny and Alissa. They smiled and seemed glad for the company. "Ready for choir tour?" I asked them. I'd decided that even if I wasn't going on the tour, I would be mature about it and not sulk.

Danny looked at Alissa. "*I'm* ready, except . . . well, Alissa can't go."

Alissa explained, "Yeah, things are changing for my family and me. We're moving next week."

"You are?" I said, startled to hear this news. "How come?"

"My dad's being transferred to another state." She and Danny looked sadly at each other.

While I talked with Danny and Alissa, I observed Andie talking and flirting with Jared. Worst of all, he was enjoying it. Once I even saw him reach over and ruffle her hair playfully. This was too much!

When I finished my dessert, I excused myself and headed to my locker. Inside, I was a wreck, upset at myself for trusting Jared. And furious with Andie for moving in on *my* territory.

Andie came careening around the corner. "Look out!"

she screeched, dropping a load of books on the floor in front of her locker.

"Watch where you throw things," I said, sidestepping her hefty stack.

"These are Jared's and mine *together*." She huffed and puffed and opened her locker.

"Where's Jared now?" I asked.

"Waiting for me on the steps," she said, pointing down the hall.

"You just couldn't stay away from him, could you?" I snapped. "I'm gone for a couple of days, and—"

"We're starting where we left off in the hospital, before *you* messed things up. Jared said so."

"He's insane," I mumbled into my locker.

"That was so dumb what you wrote on his cast," she said.

"I'll write whatever I want," I said, kicking my locker shut.

"When *I* signed his cast, Jared's hand touched mine and he whispered, 'Does this mean we're going together?' " Her eyes glazed over. "Isn't that romantic?"

I could've told her those were his exact words to *me*. Of course, she wouldn't believe me, not for a single second. So I didn't waste my breath.

Thinking back to my efforts to spend a little forbidden time with Jared at the ski lodge, I wanted to kick myself for sneaking out of the house, lying to Mom—not to mention getting grounded. And what for? To play checkers by the fire with a complete jerk? Turning away from Andie, I dashed down the hall. I couldn't get away fast enough.

"Holly, you owe me money for Bearie-O," she called

after me. "The fur's worn off his head. I could overlook it for a couple of tens."

I quickened my pace, ignoring her. I wasn't sure who I disliked more—Andie or Jared.

♥　♥　♥

Tuesday night Mom drove me to my first youth group meeting at church. Now that I was thirteen my attendance there was like some sort of debut. Definitely a big deal. Pastor Rob introduced me to all the kids and everyone clapped. Danny and Alissa sat together, grinning at me. Andie arrived late, and she walked right over and squeezed into the seat next to Jared. I sat with some new kids on the other side of the room.

After the service, I was heading down the hallway when Mr. Keller, the choir director, came out of his office. "Holly!" he said. "You're just the person I was looking for."

He ushered me into his office, and I sat down. Perching on the edge of his desk, he explained that he needed an alternate singer for the tour to take the place of Alissa Morgan, who was moving. "You have a fine voice, Holly, but I didn't choose you earlier because you were a bit younger. I wanted to give some of the older kids first dibs. However, now that Alissa is leaving, I need you. Can you attend all the rehearsals and catch up a little at home, as well?"

To sing in the youth choir I'd do anything! But then I remembered Daddy and his airplane tickets. I hesitated.

"Is there a problem?" he asked.

"Might be," I said, still surprised at this fabulous turn of events. "How soon can I let you know?"

"Two days. There are kids who would trade places with you in a flash."

When Mom came to pick me up, I told her the fantastic news. "What'll I do?" I moaned. "Will Daddy understand if I don't visit him?"

"You'll have to decide that," she said.

Carrie piped up. "You don't *really* know him, anyway."

"Speak for yourself," I shot back.

"Girls," Mom scolded. Then she said, "Holly-Heart, what about talking to the Lord about this? Pray for His guidance?"

Praying. Hmm. Something I should've thought of.

At home, I went to my room and knelt at my window seat. It felt good talking to God about everything. Again.

Then I thought of Daddy. I needed to tell *him* about the choir tour, as well. Mom was tucking Carrie into bed, so I went to her room to use the phone. It rang four times. When I heard his voice, I said, "Daddy, it's Holly. Something's come up." I told him about the choir-tour opening.

"That's wonderful news." He sounded excited.

"There's only one problem," I said.

"What's that?"

"The tour is during spring break."

There was a short pause. "I guess we could plan your visit for another time." Disappointment seemed to leap into his voice.

"What about this summer?" I suggested.

"Sure, that's a possibility." His voice revved up a bit.

"The tour will take us to L.A. So maybe you can come hear us sing during spring break."

"You can count on it. We'll be there."

We'll . . . That meant I'd have to share him with Saundra. Even the way he pronounced her name gave me the creeps. Could prayer change my attitude toward her?

I wandered downstairs, looking for Mom. She was in the family room, curled up reading a book. "Daddy said he'd come to hear me sing with the choir . . . and he agreed that maybe I could visit him this summer instead."

Mom merely nodded. "We'll talk things over."

"By the way, where's Carrie's last report card?" I asked.

"In the desk in my room. Why do you want it?"

I sat down beside her on the couch. "I thought Carrie could send it to Daddy. I feel funny about Carrie being left out of things with him. She's his daughter, too."

"How does *she* feel about it?" Mom asked, reaching over to loosen the pink clips in my hair.

"I'm not sure. I hope she doesn't feel jealous. Jealousy is a miserable thing."

Mom paused. "Now that your father has shown an interest again, maybe Carrie will want to know him better, too." She brushed one side of my hair while I did the other.

"Why didn't Daddy keep in touch with us more than just a note on a birthday card or tons of presents at Christmas?" This question burned inside me.

"Honey, I don't understand that, either. But I *do* know he has paid his support money to the court registry faithfully every month all these years. That's something lots of Dads don't do."

She braided my hair in one thick braid.

"It's still so hard," I said, deep in thought, "but I'm more concerned with his salvation now." It was true. Very few nights had passed recently that I didn't say his name in my prayers.

"I feel very close to you tonight, Holly-Heart," Mom said, giving me a hug.

"Me too." Again, I felt sorry for Stan, Phil, Mark, and little Stephie. "Mom?" I said, thinking of their loss.

"Yes, honey?"

"I really do love you. Even though I can get sassy sometimes . . . always remember?"

"I'll remember." She hugged and kissed me, and I headed for bed.

♥   ♥   ♥

At Wednesday night choir rehearsal, I was assigned a spot on the risers. Next to Jared! I couldn't believe it. I wanted to lash out at him, but I kept my mouth shut except to sing, my hands firmly gripped on the music folder.

"What a relief," Jared said between the first and second songs. "You're here. It's like a miracle."

"The only miracle I know is you haven't been found out before now," I blurted out.

"What do you mean, Holly-Heart?" He sounded so innocent.

"Don't call me that." I felt sick inside. Crushed. And fooled into thinking he was too good to be true.

We practiced five more songs for our tour repertoire before Mr. Keller dismissed us. Andie came right over to Jared, ignoring me. She acted like a mother hen, holding his crutches, helping him with his jacket.

I couldn't watch this. In the strongest voice I could muster I said, "Jared, you're not welcome at my birthday party. I've thought about this a lot, and I'm sorry." Heading for the church foyer, I waited for Mom, holding my breath and willing the tears away.

♥   ♥   ♥

On Thursday morning I got up really early. Quietly, I pulled a purple folder out from between the box springs and mattress of my canopy bed. I'd told Andie about destroying our original Loyalty Papers, but she didn't know there was a duplicate copy.

It was time to confront Andie with the truth about Jared. I cut out the paragraph referring to one of us backing away from a guy to save our friendship. In a hot pink marker, I circled it and wrote, *"I'm willing. Jared's not worth the destruction of us!"*

There, that should speak loud and clear. I folded it neatly and slipped it into a business-sized envelope. Licking it shut, I labeled the envelope, *IMPORTANT! PRIVATE!* I would slide it into her gym locker during warm-ups.

With my birthday party only three days away, things just had to work out between Andie and me. And soon.

On the snowy walk to school, I couldn't stop thinking about Andie. Would she accept my note? What could I do to make her see what a two-timer Jared was?

I was heading up the sidewalk to school when I heard someone call my name. I turned to look.

It was Jared. He sat on the brick wall surrounding the courtyard leading to the school's main entrance. His bum leg was sticking out, supported by one crutch. In his hand lay a single long-stemmed rose. "Holly-Heart," he called again. "This is for you." He held it out.

"Give it to Andie," I shot back.

He ignored that. "I know it's a little late, but happy birthday. And . . . I'm sorry about your aunt."

"Not sorry enough." I folded my arms.

"I know what you're thinking," he said. "But things aren't the way they seem." He shifted his bad leg off the crutch.

"You must think I'm totally dense, Jared. I don't want any of your explanations. What you did was unforgivable. I thought you were better than that." I turned to go.

"Honestly, Holly, Andie and I are *just friends*," he

insisted, holding the rose out farther.

"Is that what you told her about me?" I glanced around. "Where is she, anyway?"

Jared frowned. "What's wrong?"

"Nothing's wrong with me. You're the one with a problem." I remembered, with a twinge of pain, how perfect things were . . . just a week ago, *before* I'd left for Aunt Marla's funeral. The outside temperature added to the cold, painful reality of seeing Jared for who he really was. I shivered, pulling the collar of my coat against my neck.

"C'mon, Holly." He held the sweet-smelling rose out to me again. "I want you to have this."

The rose—his attention—was so hard to resist. But I had to. "Don't do this," I pleaded, turning to go, leaving him sitting alone. Opening the doors to the school, I refused to look back.

♥ ♥ ♥

During P.E. I found time to slip back down to the girls' locker room. Quickly, I opened my locker and found the long envelope with the copy of the clipping from the Loyalty Papers. I hurried to Andie's locker and slid the envelope through the slits in the door. *Now* she'd have something to think about. Maybe she'd even call me and request a face-to-face meeting. I was desperate to get my best friend back!

After school, I noticed Jared in the stairwell. He'd cornered some girl. I couldn't see who, but it wasn't Andie. Whoever it was, I could tell they were involved in animated conversation.

Way to go, Jared. Fool someone new. Peering around the corner at them made me hurt all over again.

Billy Hill zipped past, nearly knocking me over. "Excu-use me," he said. Together, we walked toward the front entrance. "You look depressed."

"It's Jared. Mr. Flirt himself is attempting to charm yet another girl," I said, referring to the stairwell scene. "Why did *I* fall for his empty words?"

"Don't be hard on yourself," Billy said, "Jared's just some guy, that's all."

"But he's two-timing Andie. If she only knew!"

"If I were Jared, I'd stick with Andie," he said, and then, realizing he'd let something personal slip, he blushed.

He likes Andie! I thought. Perfect. I shifted my books from one arm to the other.

"The way Jared was talking in class, you'd think he was stringing you along, too." Billy was covering his tracks.

I scuffed my shoe as hard as I could. "His brain's definitely warped."

Just then a fabulous idea struck. "Wouldn't it be fun to catch Jared at his own game? You know, teach him a lesson?"

"Yeah," Billy laughed. "Like how?"

We pushed the front doors open. The smell of woodsmoke filled the air.

"I have an idea, but let's talk later," I said. We headed home in opposite directions.

Cutting through the school yard, I noticed Marcia Greene making fresh footprints in the snow. She wore a heavy tan parka. The hood was tied tightly, framing her face, and in her mittened hand she had a single long-stemmed red rose.

So *that's* who Jared had cornered. Marcia Greene and I were destined for a heart-to-heart talk. Andie, too. Wait'll *she* heard about this—precisely what I needed to convince Andie of the truth. I decided to wait until after supper to phone her. That would give her a chance to get finished with homework before I dumped the bad news on her.

When I got home from school, Carrie had stacks of artwork and old report cards piled on the table. She must've heard about my chat with Mom last night. That Daddy might like to see some of her little-girl progress.

"Carrie," I called to her, opening the fridge.

She bounded up the stairs and into the kitchen. "You're home. Good."

"Want to make a package to send to Daddy?"

She showed off two pages of artwork. "These are my favorites. Think he'll like them?"

I nodded. "If you want to keep the originals, Mom can make color copies at work."

Carrie seemed to like the idea. So I spent the rest of the afternoon helping her compose a letter to Daddy.

After our supper of chicken chow mein—yum!—I settled down at the dining room table to do some homework. I was finishing up my algebra assignment when the phone rang. I flew across the kitchen to get it.

"Hey, Holly." It was Billy.

"Hey," I said.

"I was thinking about what you said today. I saw this show on TV about a guy who wasn't happy unless he was dating at least two girls at once."

"And?"

"He not only two-timed every girl he went with, but he

got messed up trying to keep things straight with the girls he'd lined up dates with."

"That won't happen to Jared," I said, determined. "Not when the word gets out about him to every girl in Dressel Hills. Beginning with Andie." I took a deep breath. "I have a fabulous scheme. Wanna help me pull it off?"

"Absolutely," Billy said.

"Here it is." I told him what I'd dreamed up on my way home from school.

Billy laughed when he heard my plan. "You're right," he said. "Your birthday party will be the perfect place to set Jared up. Whoa, Holly, you're good."

"So . . . I'll talk to you later." Excitement jitters were building inside me. I could hardly wait for the perfect moment to get Jared good.

After I hung up, I grabbed my notebook of secret lists. There were important details to plan, involving Andie, Marcia Greene, and Jared.

First, I phoned Marcia. She seemed a little hesitant, maybe a teeny bit taken in by Jared's attention (the rose probably did it), but she was willing to go along with the plan . . . for a price. I had to let her wear my purple-and-pink jacket to some ski party next week.

I agreed. That was easy.

Next, I called Jared. He seemed surprised but thrilled that I'd changed my mind about including him at my party. I didn't tell him *who* was coming, of course.

Getting Andie to show up at my party would be much more difficult. I called her last.

"Hey. It's Holly. Please don't hang up," I said.

"What can *you* possibly say that I'd want to hear?" she said sarcastically.

Praying for courage, I said, "Andie, I really want you to come to my party Saturday night."

She hesitated. "Uh, I don't know."

"Did you find the note I stuck in your locker with the clipping from the Loyalty Papers?" I persisted. "Did you read it?"

"Sort of, but I'm not—"

"*Jared's* coming to the party. I thought you'd want to come with him." It was my last ploy.

"Okay . . . sure, I'll be there. But don't expect me to share him."

I stifled the urge to do backflips. "Perfect," I said. "I'll see you Saturday night."

We said good-bye. Then I clenched my fists and jumped up and down. Mom looked at me funny when she came through the room hauling the vacuum cleaner and its attachments.

I picked up the long vacuum hose. "Here, let me help."

"Looks like we have spiders again," Mom said, waving her feather duster in the corner of the ceiling and whisking away a few cobwebs.

I shivered at the thought of the creepy things. "I don't see any spiders now," I said, fluffing up the sofa pillows.

"Not now maybe, but the proof's in the webs they spin."

It sounded like a bit of poetry and reminded me of the miniwebs I hoped to spin for Andie this Saturday night. To help her see the truth. At last!

♥　♥　♥

Friday after school Billy walked me home. "Your plan

to expose Jared is so cool," he said, stomping the snow off his boots.

"If we all do our part, it should come off like vanilla pudding." Then I set things straight with Billy. "This whole thing is *not* about revenge, just so you know. It's about getting my best friend back."

"And there's no way it won't work. You and Andie will be friends again by tomorrow night, you'll see." His smile was so big I was curious about *his* motive.

At choir rehearsal Saturday morning I went out of my way to be nice to Jared, which wasn't easy. After all, I had been nuts about him last week. The wounds from his deception were still fresh.

"Thanks for inviting me to your party," he said, sliding over on the riser to make room for me. "I thought you didn't want me to come."

"I changed my mind." I didn't say I'd had a change of heart. That would've been a lie.

Mr. Keller chose several kids to sing in an a cappella group. Danny Myers was one of the tenors. I listened as they sang, admiring Danny's performance.

After choir, Mr. Keller congratulated us on our good blend. "When we achieve unity with our voices, our music is that much stronger—more powerful. The same is true in our Christian walk when, as brothers and sisters in Christ, we have unity of mind and heart. United, we can accomplish more for the kingdom of God."

I thought about his words. Even though we were both Christians, there hadn't been much agreement between Andie and me lately. I hoped my plan would help restore some of that unity—and give me back my best friend.

16

Pastel streamers and paper cut-outs dangled from the ceiling of the dining room, creating a festive atmosphere for my birthday party. The table was covered with Mom's special white-lace tablecloth. Pink napkins were lined up beside pink plastic bowls. In the middle of the table, there were ten kinds of ice-cream toppings: strawberries, caramel, butterscotch, hot fudge, chocolate sprinkles, nuts, gummy bears, sliced bananas, maraschino cherries, and—best of all—whipped cream.

Mom rearranged the silverware, lining the forks up symmetrically. "We're all set, Holly-Heart," she said. "Why don't you go get yourself ready?"

I stood back and surveyed the table. "It's beautiful, absolutely beautiful." Impulsively, I hugged Mom. "Thanks."

"Hurry along, now," she said, chuckling like it was *her* party!

I rushed upstairs and slipped into new jeans and a hot-pink oversized wool sweater with a white dress T underneath. Then I went into the bathroom to do my hair. I brushed it vigorously, then parted it down the middle and made two big braids, one on either side of my head.

I finished the outfit off with a light-pink bandanna tied around my head.

At seven o'clock sharp, the doorbell rang. I greeted my first guests, Joy and Shauna, two girls from home ec class. Two boys from the basketball team showed up next. Later, Jared and Andie arrived . . . together. I smiled and welcomed them, but neither of them could look me in the eye. I offered them seats in the living room, where the other kids waited for the ice-cream bonanza.

The doorbell rang again. I hurried to get it.

"Billy!" I gasped. "What happened to you?"

Billy, his right leg in a cast and crutches under his arms, wobbled into the living room. Marcia Greene followed close behind, watching him and holding his arm so he wouldn't slip.

Everyone circled Billy, firing questions at him. "Clear the way," I said. "Let him sit down." I led Billy to a chair and propped his leg on a footstool.

"How's that?" I asked, sneaking a look at Jared. He was sitting next to Andie on the couch, wearing a puzzled look.

"It was a skiing accident," Billy told us. "Yesterday morning. I was skiing fast down a black slope when I hit this mogul and boom—I wiped out." He described how his sister had screamed, how the ski patrol had taken him down on the snowmobile. "Lucky my mom's a doctor. She made sure I didn't go into shock," he said.

I stole another look at Jared. He was listening to Billy with interest. *So far, so good.*

"Ice cream's ready," Mom called.

All of us trooped into the kitchen, where my mother, the perfect hostess, announced the flavors. We lined up at the kitchen bar, and Mom dished out the ice cream. Then we gathered at the dining-room table and picked out our favorite toppings.

Andie hovered near Jared. "What ice cream would you like?" she asked. "I can get it for you."

Marcia did the same. "Oh, Billy," she said. "Just tell me what you'd like on your sundae, and I'll take care of it."

A few minutes later Andie picked up the can of whipped cream. "Would you like some?" she asked Jared.

When she finished with the can, Marcia reached for it. "Billy," she said, her voice a tad sweeter than Andie's, "would you like some of this?"

"Sure, thanks," he said, playing the part.

Andie turned cherry-red. Jared frowned.

Everyone stood around the dining room, laughing and talking as we ate our huge sundaes.

Then Billy motioned for me. Balancing on his crutches, he held his punch cup high in the air. "Here's to the birthday girl," he announced. Then he blew me a kiss. I giggled. All part of the act. Jared's eyes nearly popped out.

After Mom offered seconds on ice cream, we headed downstairs to the family room while Mom and Carrie cleared away the dishes. Tossing our shoes off, my friends curled up on the sectional facing the entertainment center, and I started a DVD, pre-approved by Mom. On the coffee table stood a tall white vase displaying a single, long-stemmed red rose, which I'd bought for myself that afternoon.

The video was one of my favorites: *Ever After.* So romantic and sweet. But I hardly paid attention. I kept watching Andie and Jared. The room was dimly lit, but I thought I saw him reach for her hand. I pulled on my hair, nervous about what Billy and I had schemed to do.

The end of the video, when the credits came up, was Billy's cue. As soon as I pressed Rewind on the remote and turned on the lights, he whipped out a blue marker and asked everyone to sign his cast. When Marcia signed it, LOVE, MARCIA G., he grabbed her hand and said, "Does this mean we're going together?"

She stuttered, acting the part flawlessly. "I . . . I'll have to ask Jared," she said, facing him, while Andie's eyes popped.

There was a long, awkward silence. Jared's jaw flinched nervously.

Then Andie leaped up. "What's going on?" she said, scowling first at me, then Marcia. "Jared and I are together. What's this about?"

By now Jared looked like a trapped rat. And nearly speechless. He mumbled, "I . . . uh . . . I don't . . ."

Marcia stared at Jared and poured it on. "I thought you and I were going together, Jared. Isn't that what the rose was for?"

Andie let out a tiny gasp. She swung around to face . Jared, face aghast. I'd never known Andie to be tongue-tied, but at this minute, she was absolutely silent.

Now it was *my* turn. I picked up the dainty rosebud vase. Holding it high, I said, "Roses are usually given to represent something important. Like true friendship or . . . love. This rose is exactly like the one Jared tried to give me. But I didn't take it." I stared at Andie, hoping she could take note of my demonstration of loyalty.

"Jared gave a rose to *me*, too," Marcia declared, "after school."

"This is nuts!" Andie looked from Marcia to me and back again. "I'm outta here." Her eyes shot fire—at me.

"Meet me upstairs, Holly," she said coldly. It sounded like an invitation to a duel.

I followed her upstairs to the hall closet, where she dragged out her jacket and put it on. She pulled me outside into the bitter night. Standing there on the front porch, lit only by the faint glow of a distant streetlight, we faced each other. "What are you trying to prove, Holly *Heartless?*" she asked.

"I'm sick of Jared coming between us. Honestly, I thought this was the only way to show you what he's really like. I doubt that Jared would fill you in on how he offered me a rose, then gave it to Marcia instead. He's a two-timer, Andie. It's obvious."

"I don't care!" she said.

"You're actually going to stick with him?"

She just glared at me.

"What about our friendship—years of great times, sharing our deepest secrets, a good, solid relationship . . . the best I've ever had," I said, hoping she'd snap out of it. Hoping . . .

"You humiliated me, Holly." Her voice was shaking, and I thought I saw tears glistening in her eyes. "Our friendship's over. No more Loyalty Papers, no more teddy bears, no more nothing. You can forget about me, Holly Heartless, because this is the last time I'll ever set foot in your house."

Before I could say more she turned to leave, running full speed down our driveway and across the street.

"Andie!" I called. "Please don't leave like this."

It was a long, cold three blocks to her house, but she

kept going. Her figure rounded the corner and disappeared at the end of Downhill Court.

I shivered uncontrollably. My fabulous plan had totally backfired. What could I do now?

Downstairs in the family room, I found the boys cutting through Billy's cast with the small hacksaw I'd hidden behind the TV for this purpose.

"Guess I don't need this anymore." Billy tossed the cast aside.

"Where'd you get it?" Joy asked, eager to know.

"My mom's a doctor. She did a good job of making me look really hurt."

Staring at the signatures on the discarded cast, I felt sick inside. The scheme had blown up in my face. And Andie and I were as far removed as east and west.

Jared? He was nowhere to be seen now. Missing . . . in my house somewhere?

"He's hiding out in the bathroom," Billy said when I asked. "We sure did a number on him, don't you think?"

"It wasn't him I was after," I whispered, wishing this night had never happened. It was obvious the party was over. I thanked Marcia Greene for her fabulous dramatic presentation as she left the house. Billy too.

Then, going back downstairs, I vented my frustration by yanking down all the streamers. At last, Jared came out of the bathroom, like a turtle emerging from its shell.

He picked up the vase with the rose and leaned his nose deep into the flower. "Too bad, isn't it?" he said.

I tossed a crumpled wad of crepe paper to the floor. "No kidding."

"A rose is a symbol of love," he continued. "The Bible says we should love everyone, right? I'm doing the best I can to be a loving Christian."

I wanted to choke. Was this guy for real?

"Jared, just go home. You're leading girls on, and that has nothing to do with God's love." I threw his jacket at him and pointed to the stairs.

He flashed me a wink and a grin. "See ya, Holly-Heart."

He never quits, I thought, going in search of Mom. She was in bed, propped up with a zillion pillows, reading a magazine. When she saw me, she patted the bed beside her. I snuggled in and shared the entire dreadful evening with her.

"You embarrassed Andie in front of her classmates," Mom chided. "How else would you expect her to react?"

I nodded. "It was a lousy mistake. I didn't think about how *she'd* feel, only how lonely I felt." I pulled my socks off and threw them one at a time across the room. "Now what'll I do?"

Mom slipped her arm around me. "Only one thing, Holly-Heart. Apologize."

She was right. "It won't be easy," I said. "And Andie might not forgive me."

Mom squeezed my hand. "Oh, I don't know. Given time, you might be surprised what Andie will do."

I returned to my own bedroom, where I dressed in my

nightshirt and read my devotional. Lying in the darkness, I replayed the events of the party in my mind. Over and over, I recalled Andie's reaction. What a horrid thing I'd done. How could she ever forgive me?

♥ ♥ ♥

At church on Sunday, my conscience still pricked at me. How could I have done such a terrible thing to my best friend? I listened carefully when our pastor spoke of forgiveness of sins, and I said a silent prayer of thanks to God that He had already forgiven me. Now if I could only get Andie to do the same.

I searched right away for Andie after the service, finding her alone in the choir room. She sat at the piano, numbering measures in her music.

Standing behind the piano, I was silent for a moment. Then I said, "I'm sorry about last night, Andie. Can you ever forgive me?"

She looked up, a hint of sadness in her eyes. "Sure, Holly. I forgive you. But you should know that Jared and I are already back together."

Not surprising. Jared's charisma was hard to resist.

She went on. "He apologized to me, too. And to Marcia Greene. Jared's trying to be more up front with me now. He just wants to be good friends with *all* the girls. Really."

Some joke. If only she knew how Jared had flirted with *me* last night after everyone left. But it was pointless. She'd never believe it.

I sighed. "I hope you two get along all right." With nothing more to say, I left the room. At least she and I were talking again. But we couldn't possibly be close friends. Not until Jared Wilkins was out of the picture.

♥ ♥ ♥

February fizzled, and March piled snow on us until I thought winter might never end. I spent most of my free time with Marcia Greene. And even though Andie and I didn't talk much, at least we were civil to each other. She continued to help Jared with his crutches and his books, standing sentinel at his locker to assist him with his every whim.

The second week in March, Jared had his cast removed. To celebrate, Andie decorated his locker door with colorful balloons. I congratulated him, hoping that now that he could walk without crutches, Andie and I could resume our friendship.

But nothing seemed to change. She stuck by him as closely as before. And worse, Jared kept trying to flirt with me! At choir practices, in English class, at church. Even though I didn't respond, he kept it up.

At last it was Saturday, March twenty-seventh—the final choir rehearsal before we left for our tour on Monday. After numerous dress rehearsals in February, the choir had gone into a slump, but Mr. Keller was going to present a unified choir or die trying. We prayed at the beginning of rehearsal, as usual. Then he said, "Let's chat." He motioned for us to sit on the risers. "Some of you are still thinking in terms of solo work. In a choir situation"—and here he waved his arms to include all of us—"we must have togeth-erness. We're a group of singers, not thirty different people doing our own thing. So blend. Listen to each other. The theme of our tour is 'Hearts in One Accord.' When we sing in each of the churches on the tour, the audience must feel our inspiration, our love for the Lord, and for each other." A couple kids snickered. "C'mon, kids, you know what I mean."

I glanced at Andie, who was sitting at the piano. She, of course, was gazing at Jared, next to me. *She must really care for Jared*, I thought sadly.

Mr. Keller continued. "Acts 2:46 says, 'Every day they continued to meet together in the temple courts. They broke bread in their homes and ate together with glad and sincere hearts, praising God and enjoying the favor of all the people.' " He asked for hands. "Let's have some input from you. What's this verse mean?"

Hands shot up.

"Yes, Danny?"

"The early Christians were in agreement. They were united."

"Exactly," Mr. Keller said. "More ideas?" He pointed to Jared.

"They looked forward to pigging out together?"

The kids laughed.

Mr. Keller nodded. "But wasn't it more *how* they broke bread together?"

I raised my hand. "They were together in everything. Like best friends."

"Now we're getting somewhere," he said, rubbing his hands together. "Think about what Holly said as we rehearse the last stanza of page forty-four."

I thought about Andie sitting there at the piano as we sang. I missed her terribly. More than anything, I hoped this choir tour would restore us to true friendship. This was my earnest prayer.

18

Dizzy with excitement, I stood at the back of the Los Angeles Chapel, peering through the glass separating the foyer from the sanctuary. Scarcely was there a vacant seat—each pew was filled, right up to the altar. The crowd fidgeted. Young children peeked at parents' programs, and teens whispered on the far left side, segregated from the rest. I looked over rows of heads and soon spied the red swept-up hair of Saundra. Where was Daddy?

I became aware of the nervous rustlings behind me— the other girls, straightening their apricot-colored dresses.

"Ready for the concert?" Jared, my assigned escort, whispered.

Just then, I caught a glimpse of Daddy at the drinking fountain. "Excuse me," I said, moving out of line and dashing to him.

"Holly," he said with awe in his voice. "You look simply stunning." He gave me a tight hug.

I heard the musical cue and reluctantly pulled away. "Wait for me after the concert, okay? We'll talk then." I scurried back to my appointed spot.

Jared's hand touched my back lightly as he guided me

to my place beside him. I slipped my hand through his elbow, and we were off. It felt weird walking down the aisle with him, like we were in a wedding, or worse, getting married to each other! Andie regarded us with a half-sarcastic, half-accusing look as we rounded the altar and walked up the steps.

On the platform, we located our place on the risers. Quickly, I searched the audience for Daddy, who was leaning forward slightly. His warm smile beckoned to me like a beacon in the sea of faces.

Energetically, we sang our opening song, a lively chorus, "Everybody Sing Praises to the Lord." It was a great start by the sound of the applause. Somehow, I made it through the next few songs, even though Jared kept inching closer and closer. He and Andie had worked out some exclusive thing between them, and I refused to respond to his immature behavior.

At the intermission, during the offering, Jared strolled through the lobby to me. Handsomely outfitted in his black suit over an apricot-colored shirt, he was any girl's dream.

"You're going to introduce me to your father, right?" he asked, grinning.

I stepped back. "Why should I?"

"C'mon, Holly, you know Andie and I are just—"

"I've heard it before. Just friends, right?" I interrupted.

Andie materialized out of nowhere. "Flirting again, I see," she said to *me*.

"Tell that to Jared," I said. "If you're too blind to see the truth, then you deserve him!" I hurried to the back of the foyer area. Refusing to cry, I flipped through the church's brochure, attempting to read the now blurry statement of faith.

"Holly?"

Whirling around, I found the gray-green eyes of Danny Myers looking down at me.

"Problems with Andie?" His voice had a calming effect on me. I didn't have to tell him what was wrong. The whole choir seemed to know.

My voice grew soft. "It's not her fault. She's just . . ."

"Just what?" He seemed interested. His eyes were kind—so was his face. He was older than me and more spiritual. I remembered that from the way he'd prayed even at school during lunch.

"She's being fooled," I finally said. "It makes me angry."

"Why does it bother you so much?"

I told him how close Andie and I had always been. Until now. How I preferred *one* best friend and Andie had changed all that, because of Jared.

Danny nodded and smiled as though he understood. "Sit here, Holly." He patted a chair near the deacon's room. "You can't sing with those kinds of feelings. We're here to give to people, to minister through our music. There could be people here tonight who need Jesus."

"I know," I said, tears refusing to dry up. I was thinking of one of those people. Daddy. The gospel message we sang was for him. "I can't go back in there at all," I mumbled through my tissue. "Not looking this way."

"Let me pray for you."

I blinked the stubborn tears away.

"And we'll pray for Andie, too," he said. "She *needs* your friendship again. Can you forgive her?"

"In my heart, I can. Outside, it's not so easy."

Danny prayed a quiet prayer, full of assurance. It

touched my heart. And as the choir lined up for the second half, I felt confident again.

I thrilled to the melodies we sang—slow hymns and fast gospel songs. Lost in the music, I watched Mr. Keller's every move. During the last song, I saw Daddy reach for his handkerchief. He wiped his eyes. It was the first time I'd seen him cry. A lump came to my throat. Could this concert be a new beginning for him? The answer to my prayers?

♥ ♥ ♥

The church was nearly empty by the time all the equipment was carried out to the bus. Daddy and I were still talking in the second row. Saundra had politely disappeared a half hour before.

Daddy held my hand as he spoke. "So much about me has changed since your aunt Marla died. Losing her has been a great shock. And losing four years of your life . . . and Carrie's, well, I just wish there was a way to catch up somehow."

I hugged him, my tears falling on his suit coat. "I've been praying for you all this time," I said.

"And I love you for it," he said quickly. "We'll have lots more to talk about when you visit this summer." He gave me another hug. "Holly, will you please tell Carrie I love her, too?"

"Those words should come from you," I said.

"The right time will come." He dug into his pocket and pulled three twenty-dollar bills from his money clip. "Here, have fun at Disneyland tomorrow on me."

Something stirred in me. It was the question I had never asked him: Why had he abandoned us? My lips formed the words, but my heart squelched them. I mustn't spoil this moment.

"Thanks," I said, staring at the money. I loved *him*, not what he could give me.

"I'll give you a call when you get back from tour," he said.

"Okay," I answered. One last quick hug, and he was gone.

Staring at the empty pew beside me, I wondered why things had to be this way. If only Daddy hadn't remarried. I crossed my arms and bent over, hugging myself. The old, familiar ache of his absence had returned.

The towering pinnacles of Sleeping Beauty's Castle loomed into view as our bus rumbled to a stop near the entrance to the Magic Kingdom. Mr. Keller gave some last-minute instructions. "Above all," he warned, "remain in twos. Girls with girls, and boys with boys. Stay with your partner everywhere you go."

Danny flashed a grin at me. I knew he was saying, *Go for it, Holly. Forgive your friend.* Most girls would have loved to have an attractive older-brother type like Danny Myers. He was perfect.

I leaned over the seat behind Andie. "Wanna be my partner?" I asked.

"Why not," she grumbled. "Everyone else already has one."

Inside the main gate, we raced to Splash Mountain first. The line was long, but just hearing the screams of delight (or was it terror?) as people came hurtling down the fifty-foot drop-off, doing forty miles an hour in those little log boats, told us it would be worth the wait.

So, here we were moving along the ramp, about to go on a "must-do" fabulous ride together, and we weren't even talking. And Andie was being a real pain about it, too, keeping her back to me the whole time.

I opened my backpack. "Want some gum?" I asked.

"Is it cinnamon?" she asked.

"Spearmint." I held it out.

"Never mind." She wrinkled up her nose. "Save my place. I want to get something to eat."

My heart sank. What more could I do? Was I trying too hard?

My journal was tucked away in one corner of my backpack. So while Andie ran off to get some food, I wrote Proverbs 17:17 in my secret notebook. "A friend loves at all times." *Hmm*, I thought, *that means I should keep showing Andie I care about her, even though she's being an impossible brat.*

Soon, Andie was back with a hot dog, chips, and pop. She ignored me more than ever, talking to the girl *ahead* of us instead of me.

Forty-five minutes later, we staggered out of our log boat, having just flown down Chickapin Hill and survived.

"Wanna go again?" I asked, hoping Andie might respond.

"Maybe later," was all she said.

Undaunted, we backtracked to Astro Orbitor, a new ride at the entrance to Tomorrowland. Tucked into small "rockets," we circled around planets and other riders. Then we hit the Indiana Jones Adventure, trying to decode the markings along the wall as we moved along the ramp.

Next, Andie and I lined up for some spooky fun at the Haunted Mansion.

Then I spotted Jared. He was across from us, on the docks of the river rafts, sitting with his partner and sharing sodas with two sopranos. I watched as he worked his magic.

"Look over there," I said, pointing at Andie's two-timing friend.

"What?" Andie turned to look. She spotted Jared with the girls, and her face fell.

Silently, we watched as he teased one of them, a pretty soprano named Amy-Liz. One of the cutest girls on choir tour, Amy had curly blond hair and sparkling blue eyes. Jared's foot, newly released from its cast, reached out under the table and touched hers. She giggled and pulled back a little—but not too much. Then his foot found hers again.

"They're playing footsie!" Andie screeched. "I don't believe this."

She ducked under the roped ramp and marched over to Jared. Dying to hear what she would say, I followed.

"Jared!" she called to him.

He spun around, a guilty look on his face. But as soon as he saw Andie he grinned, bowing low. "Andie, my lady."

"Cut the comedy act," she said. "What do you think you're doing?" Andie glared at Amy-Liz.

"Spreading Christian love," he said as the girls giggled behind him.

"Wrong answer. Try this: You're two-timing every girl, everywhere, all the time!"

"I kept telling you, Andie, we're just friends, right?" He turned to Amy-Liz. "Just like Amy-Liz and me." Laughing, he took her hand and they left the table.

"You just wait," Andie hollered at him. "Every girl in Dressel Hills is going to hear about you. I promise!"

He waved without turning around.

"He should apply for the Disney court jester, don't you think?" I said.

There was disgust written all over her face. No tears, no

jealousy, just plain old disgust. The light had dawned at last.

"Jared's out. He and I are through," she announced, studying me momentarily. "Holly, can you forgive me for everything? I mean, *everything*?"

I had been waiting for this moment. "Hallelujah! The loathsome nightmare is past, and I've regained my long-lost best friend."

"Speak English, would ya?" she said, giggling. This was it. The old Andie was back.

"Look up there," I said, pointing. "Let's celebrate our renewed friendship at the Hungry Bear Restaurant."

At once we raced up the wooden walkway. Waiting in line to order hamburgers, Andie turned me around and began to braid my hair. When we finally sat down at a table on the banks of the Rivers of America, I noticed a lumpy bump in my backpack.

"What's this?" I investigated inside.

Andie opened her bag of chips, ignoring me.

There, under my jacket, and all smashed up, was Andie's droopy-eyed teddy bear.

"Pals forever?" she said, wearing a sheepish grin.

" 'Until the final end of us,' " I quoted from our now defunct Loyalty Papers, hugging Bearie-O close.

"He's missed you, you know," she said softly. "And so have I."

My emotions soared. "I missed you, too, Andie."

She took a bite of hamburger, her eyes shining. "You're really all heart, Holly. Honest. No one else would've stuck with me this long." She leaned over and sprinkled salt on my fries.

"Believe me, I had *major* help," I said, glancing heavenward.

About the Author

Beverly Lewis remembers her "first crush." He had light, wavy hair and a heart-melting smile. And he attended the church her father pastored while she was growing up in Lancaster County, Pennsylvania.

Beverly's junior high P.E. teacher gave her a nickname just as embarrassing as "Holly-Bones." And best friends? Beverly knows all about true-blue, *best*, best friends. Hers was Sandi Kline, and although they didn't have Loyalty Papers, they *did* write secret codes. Once they even hid a few under the carpet of the seventh step leading to the sanctuary of her dad's church.

A former schoolteacher, Beverly is an award-winning, bestselling author of seventy books for children, teens, and adults. She and her husband, Dave, have three grown children and one grandchild, and live in the Colorado foothills of the Rocky Mountains.

Also by Beverly Lewis

PICTURE BOOKS

Cows in the House   Annika's Secret Wish

THE CUL-DE-SAC KIDS
Children's Fiction

The Double Dabble Surprise   Tarantula Toes
The Chicken Pox Panic   Green Gravy
The Crazy Christmas Angel Mystery   Backyard Bandit Mystery
No Grown-ups Allowed   Tree House Trouble
Frog Power   The Creepy Sleep-Over
The Mystery of Case D. Luc   The Great TV Turn-Off
The Stinky Sneakers Mystery   Piggy Party
Pickle Pizza   The Granny Game
Mailbox Mania   Mystery Mutt
The Mudhole Mystery   Big Bad Beans
Fiddlesticks   The Upside-Down Day
The Crabby Cat Caper   The Midnight Mystery

THE HERITAGE OF LANCASTER COUNTY
Adult Fiction

The Shunning   The Confession
The Reckoning

OTHER ADULT FICTION

The Postcard

The Crossroad

The Redemption of Sarah Cain

Sanctuary*

The Sunroom

October Song

*with David Lewis